D0906782

WITHDRAWN

Day
of the
Hangman

***Also by Ray Hogan
in Large Print:***

Betrayal in Tombstone
A Bullet for Mr. Texas
The Copper-Dun Stud
The Crosshatch Men
Deputy of Violence
The Doomsday Canyon
The Doomsday Marshal and the Comancheros
The Doomsday Trail
The Doomsday Marshal and the Hanging Judge
The Iron Jehu
Killer on the Warbucket
A Marshal for Lawless
The Outlawed
Ragans Law
Rawhiders

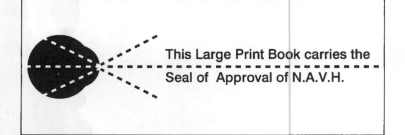

This Large Print Book carries the
Seal of Approval of N.A.V.H.

Day of the Hangman

... A SHAWN STARBUCK
WESTERN

RAY HOGAN

G.K. Hall & Co. • Thorndike, Maine

MAY 1 8 2000

Published in 2000 by arrangement with Golden West Literary Agency.

G.K. Hall Large Print Western Series.

The text of this Large Print edition is unabridged.
Other aspects of the book may vary from the original edition.

Set in 16 pt. Plantin.

Printed in the United States on permanent paper.

Library of Congress Cataloging-in-Publication Data

Hogan, Ray, 1908–
    Day of the hangman : a Shawn Starbuck western / by Ray Hogan.
        p. (large print) cm.
    ISBN 0-7838-9023-0 (lg. print : hc : alk. paper)
    1. Starbuck, Shawn (Fictitious character) — Fiction. 2. Large
type books. I. Title.
PS3558.O3473 D385   2000
813′.54—dc21
00-026760

Day of the Hangman

1

They pulled up out of the arroyo and halted. A hard grin cracked Starbuck's parched lips as he shifted his attention to the girl slumped on her horse beside him.

"I reckon we've finally made it," he said, brushing at the sweat-and-dust-clogged beard on his face.

Heather Rustin nodded wearily. "Finally," she murmured.

They had been following the smoke streamer since well before midday, certain it would lead them eventually to a settlement or perhaps a ranch, but the slender gray-blue thread that alternately thickened and faded as it twisted up into the hot, steel sky had appeared to draw no closer as the hours passed. Now, at last, they had found the source.

"Pretty fair-looking town," Starbuck said, studying the scatter of houses and buildings clustered at the far end of a flat. "Probably some ranches around here."

"Are we in New Mexico or Arizona?" the girl wondered.

Starbuck mopped at his face and neck with the palm of a hand. They had begun the day shortly before daylight, moving northeast across the upper Chihuahua Desert, and the heat even for that late October day had been brutal; now, although the late afternoon was upon them, the temperature was still high.

"Not sure," he said. "Not even certain when we crossed the border. Usually can spot a marker of some kind, but this time I never saw anything."

"But we are out of Mexico." There was a note of anxiety in Heather's voice.

A young woman only recently widowed by a band of Mexican Comancheros and held captive by them until she managed an escape and was found by Starbuck, she still had nightmarish memories of the wild, desolate country to the south.

"No doubt of that," he replied. "We've been in the saddle ten hours. Bound to be well over the line — it's just that I don't know exactly where. . . . No problem, though. We'll find out when we reach that town."

"It'll be wonderful — getting back to civilization," Heather said, sighing. "It seems ages since those outlaws attacked our wagon train . . . killed Stanley and the others."

The Comancheros had been the reason for his being in the harsh Chihuahua Desert country, too. Ben, the brother for whom he'd searched for so long, had been taken captive along with the members of the party he was riding with not long after disaster had struck the Rustin train.

In company with a squad of Mexican Federals

under command of a young lieutenant, he had pursued the outlaws, finally coming to a show-down with them in the Sierra Madre Mountains. He had been close to his long-sought meeting with his brother at that point, but then, in enabling Ben and his fellow prisoners to escape, he had been compelled to forfeit the opportunity and the anticipated end to the search he had been carrying on since he was little more than a boy.

He had wasted no time in resuming the chase, however. Knowing that Ben was striking north for the border, and only hours ahead of him, Shawn had set out in pursuit almost immediately. Lieutenant Tomas Ortiz, victorious in his desire to put an end to the activities of Choppo Valdez and his Comancheros, had generously allowed Starbuck to provision himself and Heather Rustin from his supplies before he headed back to army headquarters with the few men who had survived the encounter with the outlaws.

Starbuck had hoped the girl would accept the lieutenant's offer to return to the *presidio* with his troopers and thus leave him unencumbered as he set out to follow Ben and the others, but the young woman had refused the suggestion, making it clear she wished to continue with Starbuck.

Consequently they had headed north together, guided by the trail left by his brother and the half-dozen or so escapees accompanying him. Not effecting a meeting after getting a glimpse of Ben for the first time in many years had been a deep disappointment to Shawn, but it was no novelty.

Several times in the past he had been close, only to lose out because of a need to turn aside, lend aid to someone in need of help. Such occasions, however, had never weakened his determination to find his brother and perfect the reconciliation their father had wished for — a chore that would be completed only after he had taken Ben back to their home near the Muskingum River in Ohio so that the Starbuck estate, pending that moment, could be settled.

It had been a long, devious trail, one that wound and looped and doubled back and forth across the West in a frustrating, aimless fashion, as Ben, now calling himself Damon Friend, drifted from town to town. Shawn, who had begun the search while in his middle teens, had quickly developed into a man, one capable of many things — expert, in fact, in all the crafts necessary to stay alive, and respected, perhaps even feared to some extent, by many whose paths he chanced to cross.

He had labored as a cowhand, a bullion-wagon guard, lawman, trail boss, ranch foreman, both shotgun rider and driver for stagecoaches — a dozen other vocations during the years of search, all to the benefit of experience and the molding of his character. But such worked also as a detriment to his own future.

At times he'd grown weary of the quest, had been tempted on brief occasions to forsake it and make a life for himself, but always at the end he had ridden on, the charge given him by his dead father always having its way with him.

He still had hopes of overtaking Ben before he could again vanish into the sprawling frontier, because the trail his brother and those with him were leaving on the hot desert was plain. He felt that by riding hard, his chances were better than good that he and Heather could catch up with the escapee party by the time they reached the border.

The unpredictable Chihuahua had voided that possibility before darkness fell that first day. Another of that blistered country's fierce sandstorms had sprung up — hot, blinding, and sweeping the land clean of all marks. It had become so savage that they had been forced eventually to take shelter with the horses inside a lean-to *jacal* on the lee side of a butte to escape the cutting particles of sand. When daylight had come they looked out upon a new world, one from which all traces of his brother's passage had been erased.

But Ben and his party could have gone only one way, and that was north. Thus, with Heather and the horses as well as himself refreshed by a night's rest despite the raging storm, they had pressed on. How far ahead Ben might now be was only conjecture; he and those with him could have been beyond the storm, clear of its sweeping, yellow gusts and thus not forced to halt for fear of blinding their horses or other reasons. If true, they had undoubtedly increased their lead by many miles.

But the fact remained that they would have to cross the border somewhere ahead and point for the nearest town. It would be the only logical course to follow; thus, although the trail was lost, their immediate destination was apparent, and he and Heather had only to continue north, cross the line, and make for the nearest settlement.

Smoke had guided them to that most welcome site, and now, halted on the rim of a deep arroyo, Shawn Starbuck considered the town while they allowed the horses to rest. By all reasoning Ben would still be there; after the arduous days of captivity with the Comancheros and the long, hard ride to the border in escaping them, he'd not be in any hurry to continue on his way; undoubtedly it would be in his mind to lay over, rest.

The one possibility of such not proving to be the fact would be that Ben had crossed the border at some distant point and ended up in another town. The sandstorm had voided all chances of knowing exactly where he could have left Mexico and entered the United States, and Shawn had relied entirely on a streamer of smoke that had been visible to him as a guide. It had seemed to him on several occasions while they were riding toward it that it was leading

12

them farther east than they should be going, but he'd felt it wise to stay with it as a marker. Just where they would find another town was a question that he could in no way answer, and it seemed best to stay with a sure thing.

He turned his glance to Heather. She was staring off across the distance at the settlement, her brown eyes intent, her even features long since past the stage of sunburn and now a soft, creamy tan, smooth and settled. There was more to her than just a calm, quiet beauty, he thought, noting the way the sunlight played with her thick, honey-colored hair; she had a toughness to her, a willingness to face anything that came to oppose her, and she gave no quarter regardless of the possible consequences. Heather Rustin was quite a woman.

"Might as well ride on in," he said. "We'll get no closer sitting here."

The girl turned to him. "I guess I was dreaming, thinking about how nice it will be — a clean bed inside four walls, and a roof over my head. And good food to eat again. I don't think I realized how much I've really missed all that until now. . . . Or maybe I just never took time to think about it."

"Probably the way of it," Starbuck said, nodding. "When we get there, you check us in the hotel."

She frowned, looked at him closely. "Aren't you going to —"

"Aim to scout around a bit, ask some questions about my brother."

"Oh, yes . . . your brother," Heather said in a falling voice. "If he's not?"

"I'll have to keep on looking for him . . . but I'm hoping I'll have some luck this time."

"He'd be here if he crossed the border ahead of us, wouldn't he?"

"That's the big question. He could have come over at some other point, ended up in a different town. He and those people with him have crossed over by now — there's no doubt of that; just where's the problem. Losing their trail in that sandstorm ruined a sure thing for us."

"I hope he's here," Heather said tiredly. "If he's not, will you go right on? I was wishing that we could . . ."

Her words trailed off into uncertain silence. Starbuck's shoulders stirred.

"Rest? No reason why you can't."

"I wasn't thinking of that," she said.

He frowned. "Hardly see what else —" he began, and stopped as the flat crack of a gunshot broke the afternoon's hush.

2

Starbuck raised himself in his stirrups, seeking a better look into the town. He could see a small crowd in the street.

Heather sighed heavily. "There's some kind of trouble there, Shawn. I . . . I think we'd better ride on."

He glanced at her, surprised. "Gunshot doesn't always mean trouble."

"I know that, but after all we've been through, I don't want to see you get mixed up in something —"

"I'll manage," he said a little stiffly, and then in a softer tone added, "Next town could be a hundred miles in any direction. We've got no choice but to stop. Let's go."

Roweling the big sorrel gelding he rode lightly, Starbuck moved off toward the settlement at a slow lope and shortly reached the end of the street. With Heather close behind him, he swung onto it and angled for a narrow two-story building that stood first in the line of structures on its west side. A faded sign nailed to the wall above the porch roof bore the lettering: YUCCA FLAT HOTEL.

Yucca Flat. That apparently was the name of the settlement, he thought, as he halted at the hitch rack, but whether they were in Arizona or New Mexico he had yet to determine.

Stepping off the sorrel, he wrapped the reins about the rack's crossbar, turned to secure those of Heather's gray. The girl had already come off her saddle, was moving back into the center of the street for a better look at what was taking place. Both horses tied, Starbuck crossed to her, walking in the stiff, halting way of a man who had been too long in the saddle.

There were six hardcase-looking riders standing in front of the jail. Shoulders slouched, hats pushed to the backs of their heads, there were some with hands resting carelessly on the butts of the pistols hanging at their hips. Others had their thumbs hooked in the cartridge-filled gunbelts encircling their waists. They faced a small party of men, the town's leading citizens, apparently, from a distance of a dozen paces or so, while the remainder of the settlement looked on from porches, doorways, windows, and various other positions of relative safety along the way.

One of the riders, a lean, narrow man with a full black moustache and wearing a flat-crowned hat, raised the pistol he was holding, drove a bullet into the window of the general store. When the clatter of falling glass had ceased, he glanced about, his sharp features sardonic and cynical.

"Just want you all to know we mean business," he drawled.

Shawn, touching Heather Rustin's arm, dropped back and mounted the steps to the hotel's porch, where a small group of men and women were looking on. He nodded to a squat, thickset individual, obviously a drummer, who turned to him.

"What's this all about?"

"They're outlaws — killers," one of the women replied bitterly before the man could make an answer. "They've come after Lem Forsman."

"Who's Lem Forsman?"

"He murdered our town marshal . . . and he's one of their bunch. The judge sentenced him to hang in the morning, but they're here to stop it. Showed up just a little while ago."

"One doing the talking's Cobb Crissman," the elderly man on the porch volunteered. "He's the boss of the bunch."

"Want you all to hear me good!" The outlaw leader's voice carried throughout the street. "Nobody's lynching a friend of mine."

"He got a fair trial," someone among the men in the street said in a faintly protesting tone.

"Don't mean a damn to me — and it sure better not to you!" Crissman snapped. "Either you turn Lem over to me and the boys, or by midnight there won't be nothing left of this dump but a pile of ashes."

The outlaw raised his gun once more, threw a shot at the belfry of the church. The bell clanged loudly as the bullet smashed into it.

"Will the town do what he says?" Heather asked.

The woman who had been doing the talking shrugged. "I don't know. It's up to my husband — he's the mayor — and the council."

"Looks to me like that bunch has got your town pretty well buffaloed," Starbuck observed dryly. "Wonder they're even bothering to talk — just didn't walk into the jail and break out this Forsman."

"Not in there, that's why," another of the onlookers said, "otherwise they would've, I expect. The deputy took him out of town and hid him somewheres. Reckon he figured something like this was apt to happen, and he wanted the prisoner in a safe place until the hanging."

"Don't see any lawman out there. Where is the deputy?"

"Nobody knows. Just up and disappeared sometime last night. Some folks figure he got wind of Crissman and them coming and lit out."

"Not Dave Gallinger," the elderly man said with a shake of his head. "He's not the kind that'd run — not from nobody."

"Then where the hell is he? Ought to be out there backing up the mayor."

"Something's happened to him, more than likely. . . ."

"You mean maybe Crissman's put a bullet in his back, like Forsman done Arlie Pringle?"

"Not just my opinion. Quite a few others thinking that."

Starbuck gave that a moment's thought. Then: "The deputy the only one who knows where Forsman's hid out?" he wondered, realizing what such would mean to the town if it were true.

"Not sure," the elderly man said, "but I expect the mayor knows. Maybe the rest of the town council, too. If it was me —"

"Now, this here gent is Gabe Mather!" Crissman's ironic voice cut in. "Step up here, Gabe, let the folks get acquainted with you."

One of the outlaws, a husky, dark man with a round face, moved forward a stride. He was about the same age as Cobb Crissman — thirty or perhaps thirty-five. Doffing his dusty, stained hat in mock politeness, Mather drew his pistol, sent a bullet into the window of a building at the far end of the street.

The shot brought a woman screaming into the open, both hands clutching her face where showering splinters of glass had apparently found their mark. A man rushed out after her, gathered her in his arms, and hustled her back into the building. Starbuck, jaw hardening, drew up slowly.

Mather and the men with him laughed, snapped a second bullet at the metal stovepipe sticking out of the roof of the bakery.

"About time somebody stepped in, put a stop to this," Shawn muttered.

"Who?" the woman next to Heather demanded in a frustrated voice. "Only man who'd have enough nerve to do that, Arlie Pringle, is dead — murdered by Lem Forsman."

"Looks to me like there's plenty of other men in town, and you've got a mayor and a council who could get them all together."

"You expect them to stand up against outlaws like Crissman and them others? They're killers, ever' last one of them. Our men wouldn't have a chance."

"Ought to try," Starbuck said evenly. "The law's the law and's not something to be kicked around. Somebody had better make that plain to Crissman and his bunch."

The drummer, silent throughout it all, smiled, rubbed at his chin. "No doubt about that, friend," he said, nodding to Shawn. "Maybe you'd like to be the one."

"That's a thought," Starbuck replied crisply, and threw his glance along the buildings lining the near side of the street.

A fairly sharp bend in the roadway hid the structures beyond the jail from view, but a roof rising above all others in between supported the sign: SARGENT'S LIVERY STABLE. Pivoting on a heel, Shawn moved toward the edge of the porch.

"Wait here," he said to Heather, and stepping down onto the weedy ground, headed for the area behind the hotel.

3

From the street came the derisive voice of Cobb Crissman.

"Now, this here, ladies and gents, is Denver Jessel. Reckon he's about the most wanted galoot in the territory. He's a real tough *hombre,* folks — you can believe me. Show 'em, Denver."

A pistol cracked twice in rapid succession. A dog yelped in pain, fell silent.

Grim face set, Starbuck rounded the back corner of the Yucca Flat and quickened his step along the littered alleyway behind the buildings. Crissman was making a big show of himself and the hardcases siding him, dragging out the agony and deepening the shame through which they were putting the town's officials while enjoying each and every moment of it. If it were allowed to continue, someone, sooner or later, would be seriously injured if not killed.

Reaching a passageway lying between two of the buildings, Starbuck paused, aware of the hush that had fallen over the town. Taut, he swerved from his course directed for the livery stable and doubled back to the street. Halting at the edge of the board sidewalk, he put his attention on the roadway.

The outlaws were still below him and facing

the townsmen. There was no change in their positions. He brought his glance about, swept the storefronts, searching for signs of an injured person. JORGENSON'S FEED & SEED STORE . . . THE BORDER QUEEN SALOON . . . PURDY'S BAKERY . . . THE EAGLE CAFÉ . . . BARKLEY'S GENERAL STORE . . . two or three vacant structures. Along those buildings standing opposite him, withdrawn and deserted-looking in their moment of trial, he could note no difference from his earlier observation.

He shifted his gaze to the near side. THE YUCCA FLAT HOTEL . . . KINNEY'S HARDWARE & GUN SHOP . . . DR. WILHELM SCHULTZ . . . MARTHA'S DRESS SHOP . . . J. WHELAN, ATTORNEY-AT-LAW . . . the jail . . . SARGENT'S LIVERY STABLE . . . a few other establishments that went nameless. In front of one of those he saw the reason for the abrupt quiet. A small boy was crouched over the lifeless body of a dog.

"Now, we got us Cass Baker . . ."

Hanging onto his temper, Starbuck swung his eyes to the outlaws at the sound of Crissman's contemptuous voice.

"Expect he's the best hand with a sixgun you ever seen. Watched him once shoot the eye out of a owl that was settinz in a tall pine, without even rustling a feather! Whyn't you give the folks a little sample, Cass?"

Baker, a young blond with a boyish smile, pulled his weapon, spun it deftly on a finger, whipped it up, and emptied it into the high false

22

front of the Border Queen. Puffs of dust spurting from a small, circular area no larger than a man's hand bore proof of his expertise.

"Now, how's that, folks?" Crissman demanded, as the outlaw stepped back, began to rod the spent cartridges from his pistol and reload. "Ain't that a caution? You see who you're fooling around with?"

One of the men in the group with the mayor said something in reply to Crissman. The outlaw chief waved him off with an indifferent gesture of his hand.

"We ain't done yet, mister," he said.

Shawn wheeled, retraced his steps to the alley, and continued on for the livery stable. At that point along the street he would be below and in back of the outlaws, and in position to act — assuming he could come up with a practical idea. With six gunmen to contend with and the towns-people seemingly unwilling to make a move, he was unsure as to what he could do.

He reached the rear of the jail, crossed behind it, slowed. In the narrow lot between the square, adobe-brick, barred-window structure and the livery barn the gaunt shape of a gallows reared itself. The timbers were mostly new, unpainted, and a canvas had been stretched around the underpinning to shut off a view of the victim who was to plunge through the trapdoor to his death. The grim structure had apparently been built only recently — and expressly for Lem Forsman.

"Want you all to meet Job Roanoke." Cobb

23

Crissman's words seemed to hang in the hot, motionless air. "Old Job's prob'ly the meanest cuss on both sides of the border. Why, it keeps me and the rest of the boys plumb busy holding him down from doing all kinds of ornery things — 'specially if there's a woman around.

"Once seen him take a gal that'd acted kind of uppity with him and . . . But maybe I best not go into that right now. Just you take my word for it — he's a ring-tailed humdinger when he's riled. . . . Take yourself a bow, Job."

Roanoke was probably the oldest man in the gang, Shawn concluded as he watched from his position near the gallows. Fifty or so, he had a cold, gray look to him, and when he bent forward slightly to draw the pistol hanging on his hip, he did so with the smooth, effortless motions that came only from years of experience.

Job Roanoke did not fire his weapon, merely slipped it back into its scarred but darkly greased holster — another indication of his calling. He was a man not given to pulling his weapon except for cause, and Starbuck marked him down as probably the most dangerous outlaw of the lot.

Moving on, Shawn pointed for the wide doors in the rear of the stable that he could see beyond a corral. Circling the high post fence within which a half-dozen horses stood in slack-hipped ease as they dozed in the hot sunlight, he gained the building and entered. Hesitating briefly to let

24

his eyes adjust to the change in light, he continued, following out the wide runway that divided the stalls in the musty-smelling structure, and came finally to the front entrance. In the street outside he could hear Crissman and his outlaw companions laughing among themselves at something that had just been said.

Halting at the edge of the doorway, Starbuck threw his glance toward them. They were no more than a dozen yards away, their backs to him as they faced the sweating townsmen.

"Something I can do for you?"

Shawn caught sight of the speaker standing just outside the doorway as he turned. He was a tall man with light hair hanging well down on his neck, and a ruddy face cut by black brows and a full moustache. The clothing he wore — overalls, dark shirt, and scuffed, crusted boots — labeled him as being a part of the stable.

"You Sargent?"

The fellow nodded. "Ross Sargent — my pa ain't here no more. Been dead more'n a year. . . . Didn't hear you ride in."

"Walked. Left my horse down at the hotel."

Sargent's eyes narrowed. "You part of them?" he asked, jerking a thumb at the outlaws.

"No. Came down here where I'd get a better look at what's going on. . . . Name's Starbuck."

The livery-stable man extended his hand, swore deeply. "Sure a hell of a thing. Them bastards are whipping this town down to size for sure. You just passing through?"

"Came up from the border. Been in Mexico for a spell. What's the deal here? Isn't anybody going to do something about that bunch before —"

"This here jasper's called Stinger — Stinger Kenshaw." Crissman's words cut into Starbuck's question. "He's a right nice galoot unless he's crossed — and that's what you folks are doing to him."

The outlaw chief paused, glared at the men grouped before him. "Now, he don't take kindly to that. Ain't that right, Stinger?"

Kenshaw, a heavily built, thick-shouldered man with massive arms, wagged his head.

"It sure is, Cobb . . . and if they don't turn my *compañero* Lem loose mighty damn quick, I'm going to get real mad." Kenshaw whipped out his pistol, coolly blasted the windows of the buildings directly opposite him — those of Kinney's Hardware, the doctor's office, and the ladies' dress shop — in methodical order.

A chorus of screams and yells erupted from the interiors of the structures before the echoes of the shots had died, all of which set the outlaws to laughing again. Sargent stirred helplessly, swore.

"Goddamnit, we got to do something . . ."

Crissman, the last of the asinine, graphic introductions of his followers over, made a mock bow to the harried men facing him.

"I reckon that gets you acquainted with us and what we can do if we take the notion. Now, if

26

there's anybody that's maybe misdoubting us and would like to see the boys cut up a bit more . . ."

"No — there's no need!" one of the men in the crowd said hastily.

"That's good. We don't want to stir things up none — and we won't, long as you counter-jumpers see it our way. But if you don't . . . Well, I sure hate to think what'll happen to this here town and a lot of you folks. . . . You savvy what I'm saying?"

4

"Where'd your man go to? Don't see him nowheres along the street."

Heather Rustin made no reply to the drummer's question. Shawn was not in sight, but he was down there somewhere, probably waiting for the moment when he could act.

"You think he can do something about this?" the woman who had mentioned that her husband was the mayor asked in a worried voice.

"He'll do what he can, you can depend on that," the girl said. She was glowing inwardly; the drummer had referred to Shawn as *her man,* and it had sent a sense of pride surging through her. "I know how he feels about outlaws."

She slid a covert glance at the persons gathered on the hotel's porch: the drummer, the large woman in the calico dress who said she was the mayor's wife, an elderly, well-dressed couple, another woman wearing widow's weeds, a third man who had a large tooth from some animal dangling from a heavy gold watch chain looped across his paunch.

"He some kind of a lawman — a U.S. marshal, maybe?" the husband part of the elderly couple wondered, a hopeful note in his tone.

"No, but he has worked for the law — he's

28

been a lot of things, actually. He can do anything he sets his mind to. There've been times —"

Heather recoiled, breaking off in mid-sentence. One of the outlaws had drawn his pistol and shot a dog that had wandered out from between the buildings below them. A small boy had then appeared, hurried to the dead animal, and was crouching over it.

"Weren't no call for that," the drummer said in a low voice. "No call a'tall for shooting the kid's dog."

The widow had begun to weep raggedly, and the elderly man's wife turned to her. "It's all right, Mrs. Kovacks," she said consolingly, placing her arms around the woman. "I'm sure Mayor Teague and the councilmen will get all this straightened out."

"Ain't much they can do," the man wearing the tooth watch fob said bluntly. "That bunch has got the upper hand. . . . Goes for your man, too," he added, nodding to Heather. "He won't get no help from any of them standing around looking on."

"He knows that, I expect, and he won't be fig-uring on any. I've been through a lot with him, and I found out a long time ago he relies on him-self."

"Sure must be some kind of a man!" the drummer said in a slightly scornful tone.

"He is," the girl came back promptly. "He's been on his own, chasing about this God-forsaken country since he was no more than a

29

boy, looking for his brother, who's somewhere in this area — maybe right here in this town. That's what brought us here — that and escaping from the Comancheros."

"Comancheros? The Mexican bandits?" the drummer said.

"Yes. I was with a wagon train they captured. They made me a prisoner along with several other people. Shawn — his full name is Shawn Starbuck —"

"Sounds Indian. He a half-breed?"

"Of course not! His mother was a teacher, the same as I, who worked among the Shawnee tribe. She took his name from that."

Mrs. Kovacks had stopped her weeping, was staring at her. "Did he save you from those . . . those Comancheros?"

Heather nodded. "They'd caught his brother, too. He'd been a member of a different wagon-train party, and Shawn was following them. I got away from the man who was holding me when he got killed; then Shawn found me. He's been taking care of me ever since."

There was a lengthy silence, broken finally by the elderly woman. "Then he's not your husband?"

"Not exactly — at least, not yet," Heather said with a smile. "I'm a widow, too," she continued, glancing at Mrs. Kovacks. "My husband, Stanley, was killed when those Mexican outlaws attacked our wagon."

"You must have had a terrible time of it," Mrs.

30

Teague commented.

A fleeting moment of bleakness shadowed Heather Rustin's features, and then vanished. "I owe so much — everything, in fact — to Shawn," she murmured.

"This brother he's looking for," the elderly man said hesitantly. "Could be I know him if he lives around here."

"He wouldn't be living here," the girl said, shaking her head. "His name's Ben, but he's calling himself Damon Friend now. He and their father got into an argument and he ran off. When their father died later on, he put it in his will that Shawn had to find Ben and take him back to their home town. There's some family business that has to be settled."

"Well, if he doesn't live around here, what makes Starbuck think he'll find him in Yucca Flat?"

"He and some other people were headed this way —"

A splatter of gunshots broke into Heather's words. Mrs. Kovacks began to cry again, and the man with the watch fob muttered something under his breath as one of the outlaws emptied his pistol into the wooden facade of the saloon, the bullets all centering in a small area.

The drummer whistled. "That's the best shooting I've ever seen," he said admiringly. "You could cover all six of them holes with your hat — and at that distance, that's something! I sure wouldn't want to buck up against that bird."

31

"It was good shooting, all right," Heather agreed, recovering herself. "But I've seen Shawn do better."

The drummer grinned. "He must be a wonder. What do you reckon's happened to him?"

"I'm not worried," the girl said. "He'll show up when the proper time comes."

"That boy," Mrs. Teague said, her eyes still on the young outlaw who had just demonstrated his marksmanship, "he can't be more than sixteen, maybe seventeen. . . . It's a shame he's gone and got himself mixed up with a bunch of cutthroats like those other men."

Heather fell to probing the buildings along the street with a thoughtful gaze. There was still no sign of Shawn, but that in no way disturbed her; he would not fail to put in an appearance; she was as positive of that as she was of night following day. She wondered what he had in mind to do and how he could handle six dangerous outlaws. Whatever, he would have to do it alone, there was no doubt of that. No one in the whole town seemed inclined to stand up to the renegades; all lacked the courage, apparently.

Idly, she watched one of the gang, the sort of old-looking member, jerk out his pistol, spin it on a finger, and then return it to its holster. . . . Somewhere back of the bakery — Purdy's Bakery, the sign said — a horse whinnied, and overhead several doves, their wings whispering in flight, swept by.

Down along the sidewalk, the small boy had gathered up the body of his dog, and cradling it in his short arms, was hurrying off into the passageway that lay between the Eagle Café and its neighbor, a vacant building, pointing, no doubt, for the houses that lay beyond. Anger stirred the girl. As the drummer had said, there was no need for that outlaw to kill the boy's dog.

The older outlaw had stepped back into line with his friends, and Cobb Crissman was making his final introduction — a man he called Stinger Kenshaw. The long, dragging moments of tension were beginning to tell on the people around her, she noted. Their faces looked gray and strained, and there was a nervousness about them that betrayed their anxiety. Only the drummer seemed unaffected.

She glanced down the street, jerked involuntarily as Stinger Kenshaw, bringing his gun into play, shattered the glass windows of several store buildings just below the hotel. She could hear a man yell hoarsely, and from inside one of the shops a woman screamed in a high, distracted way.

"That man of yours better do something pretty soon if he's going to," Mrs. Teague said grimly. "If those bullets didn't hurt somebody inside Martha's Dress Shop or the hardware store, I'll be surprised."

"Seems to me you're all expecting a lot from a man that don't even live here — a stranger, in fact," the drummer said, his attitude changing.

"It's up to the town, not him."

"Was the lady that done all the bragging on him," the portly man with the tooth watch fob said acidly. "Don't recollect anybody asking him to cut himself in."

"Maybe not, but if he figures what's going on ain't right and's willing to try and stop it, rest of you ought to back him up — not just stand by and leave it all up to him."

"That include you?"

The drummer scrubbed at his jaw. "Well, I ain't no great shakes with a pistol — hardly ever shot one, in fact. And it ain't my place, either, it not being my town, but if I'm called on . . ."

"Just what I figured — big talk and nothing else. Beginning to think that goes for this fellow Starbuck, too — meaning no offense, lady."

"Just be patient," Heather replied, her confidence still unshaken.

5

Starbuck, taut with anger, listened to Cobb Crissman's insolent words and then watched one of the men facing the outlaw leader, an elderly individual dressed in a faded blue suit, checked shirt, string tie, and narrow-brimmed hat, bob hurriedly.

"Sure do."

Shawn turned to the stable owner. "He's the mayor, I take it. . . ."

"That's him," Sargent said. "Rufus Teague — runs the hotel. Rufe's a good, honest man, but he's grown old and full of fear. Expect he's doing what seems best to him."

"Best maybe, but not right. Who's that standing next to him?"

"Pete Barkley."

Starbuck pointed at the general store. "That his place?"

Sargent nodded. Barkley was a much younger man than Teague but appeared every bit as anxious to meet the outlaw's terms.

"Nobody else around here have any say in this but Teague?"

"Oh, sure. Council met, hashed it over after Crissman and his bunch rode in and laid it on the line what they wanted."

35

"When was that?"

"Around noon. I'm one of the members. Others are Jim Rowe, a rancher east of here; Barkley; and Mason Ryder — he owns the Border Queen. Was him and me that voted to tell them to go to hell, though God only knows what we would've done if it turned out Crissman wasn't bluffing. Vote was three to two in favor of handing Forsman over to them."

"What about other folks in the town? How do they feel about it?"

Ross Sargent shrugged, eyes on the outlaws. "They'll leave it up to Teague and lay low until it's all over with."

"Must be some who think enough of the law to be against this."

"A few — sure. Know Doc Schultz is for telling them to go to hell. And Asa Jorgenson. Probably others, too, but they're keeping quiet. Bunch of hardcase outlaws like that puts the fear of God into folks."

Starbuck swore. "People ought to realize that kowtowing to the Crissmans of this world, like they're doing, will only lead to more trouble. Once a gang like that gets their way, they'll never leave this town alone. They'll figure they own it and can do whatever they want. And the word will spread. Pretty quick, more of their kind will move in."

Sargent brushed impatiently at the sweat on his forehead. "Try making Teague and the others see that. It'll be the same as talking to a stone wall. All they're worried about is right now — and what could happen."

"Maybe giving in to Crissman will take care of today, but there's always tomorrow and the days after that. Yucca Flat could become a regular hangout for outlaws. I've seen it happen in other places where the law backed down — and this town, being close to the border, is just what a lot of outlaws are looking for. When things get too hot for them, they can duck over the line. . . . Any chance of getting some help from the next town?"

"Not enough time left for that. Main reason why Crissman set sundown as the deadline, I expect."

"What about the army?"

"Same answer. Post's not close enough for troopers to get here by dark."

"Seems he has it all figured out in his favor. Understand from what I heard back at the hotel that this Forsman killed your town marshal."

"Shot him in the back — was cold-blooded murder. Was plenty of witnesses."

"Was the trial held before a regular circuit judge and not just a local court?"

"Circuit judge. Just happened he was due. Rode in two days later. Everything was all legal and according to the law, if that's what you're driving at."

"That's what I wanted to know. See you got a gallows built."

"Been ready for a week. Hangman's here, too — John Leviticus by name. Makes a business of it. Judge sent him after he left. He's at the hotel, waiting."

"No reason then why the execution shouldn't be carried out."

"None," Sargent said, "except we'll never get it done — not with Cobb Crissman and the rest of Forsman's pals hanging around. . . . Not sure you savvy what kind of jaspers we're up against. They're the worst kind — killers, murderers, every one of them. They'll shoot you down without batting an eye if you get in their way."

"I've come up against their kind before," Shawn said quietly. "Long as they've got the upper hand, they're tough."

"Probably right — but changing that's the hard part of it."

"It's what has to be done. Country'll never become a decent place to live until they're stopped cold and made to understand the law's the law and not something they can tromp all over — or else are killed off."

"Won't argue against that," Sargent said wearily. "But what can we do about it? It'd take a company of soldiers to handle them."

Starbuck's attention remained fixed on the outlaws. They were talking and laughing among themselves, enjoying some private joke while Rufus Teague, Barkley, and the other men with them waited obediently in the hot sun for permission to be on their way.

"What about this deputy that nobody's seen; any chance of him showing up to take a hand?"

"Don't figure on it. My guess is he's laying out there in the brush somewhere, dead — bush-whacked. Dave Gallinger had plenty of guts. He wouldn't have ducked out because he was scared."

"Then maybe we've got two murders that can be chalked up to the Crissman bunch."

"I'd give you odds on it — and before this is over, the way they're shooting up things, there'll likely be a couple more to bury. Could be accidental, perhaps, but murder just the same."

"Makes it twice as important they be stopped — and right now."

Ross Sargent frowned, stared at Shawn. "You figuring to try to do something about it — all by yourself?"

"If that's what it takes."

"But one man against —"

"I'm banking on getting some help, once the first move is made," Starbuck said coolly. Reaching down, he pulled the holster strapped to his left thigh forward a bit. "You willing to take a hand if I start it?"

The stable owner stroked his moustache thoughtfully. "Two of us won't count for much against them, and I ain't damn fool enough to believe that being in the right is going to stop any bullets. . . ."

"No, but it helps," Starbuck countered dryly.

"Might be able to get jorgenson and Schultz, maybe a couple others to side us, but it'll take a little time."

"Something we don't have —"

A gunshot, followed instantly by a clang of the church bell, cut into Starbuck's words. Crissman, swaggering broadly, moved a few steps away from his followers. Beyond him Rufe Teague was mopping at his sweaty face with a bandanna, while Barkley and the men with him shifted about nervously in the ankle-deep dust of the street.

"Want you folks to know that it's all settled!" the outlaw chief called in a loud voice. "The mayor's going to turn Lem over to us by sundown. Said he'd be glad to do that right now, only Lem ain't here. They've gone and hid him out somewheres — leastwise, that deputy you had did.

"But that's all right. I'm forgiving you for that, and me and the boys are willing to wait a spell — till sundown — but not one goddamn minute later! You hear that? If Lem ain't here by then, things are sure going to pop, so all of you best get busy and do what you can to help the mayor."

Sargent groaned, swore helplessly. "That ties it! We'll play hell getting anybody to lift a hand to —"

"He'll be here!" Rufus Teague's voice was high-pitched, unnatural from the anxiety that gripped him.

"Then you best start hustling. Ain't long to sundown."

"Know that. I'm sending for him right away."

"You do that, Mr. Mayor," Crissman said in his offhand, caustic way. "Me and the boys'll be waiting right over there in that saloon."

6

Starbuck took a step forward. Ross Sargent reached out, seized him by the arm.

"What're you aiming to do?" he demanded anxiously.

"Uphold the law," Shawn snapped, jerking clear, and keeping in behind the outlaws, closed in quickly and quietly on Cobb Crissman.

The sardonic gunman, a bit to one side and his back to Starbuck, started to turn, make some remark to his friends. At that moment Shawn jammed the muzzle of his pistol into his spine. Grabbing the outlaw leader by the collar with his free hand, he spun him about to face the others.

"Any one of you makes a move for a gun, I'll blow him in two!" Starbuck warned, starting to retreat for the jail.

Crissman, yanked back on his heels and badly off balance, struggled to get his footing.

"What the goddamn —"

"I'm locking you up until after the hanging," Shawn replied harshly.

"Like hell you are!" Gabe Mather yelled, lurching forward.

Starbuck halted. "Hold it! You want Crissman to stay alive, you'll forget that!"

The outlaw chief winced as Shawn emphasized the words with a vicious jab of his gun barrel. Cobb Crissman's face had turned an angry red.

"Do what he's telling you," he grated, shaking his head at Mather and the other outlaws, now facing him in the glowering half-circle. "He ain't going to keep me in there long, and when I'm out, I'll do some settling up with him, personal."

Elsewhere along the street people were coming into the open, edging toward the jail. Teague and Barkley, struck dumb with surprise, were watching, mouths agape.

"Move," Starbuck ordered, jerking at Crissman's collar and setting him to stumbling backward again.

"You ain't holding him — not for a damned minute!" the outlaw named Baker declared, following slowly. "We'll be coming soon as you're inside."

"Be a load of buckshot waiting for any man that tries it," Shawn answered.

He continued backing slowly, keeping Crissman directly before him, shielding himself from Baker and the others while he maintained a relentless pressure against the man's spine with the muzzle of his weapon.

The rowel of a spur came up against the edge of the jail's landing. Stepping up, all but dragging Crissman, he entered the heat-filled office. Kicking the door shut, Shawn reached out, lifted the outlaw's pistol from its holster, and threw it into a far corner of the room. Then, pulling the man about, he shoved him roughly through the open door of the first cell off the end of the office.

Cursing wildly, Cobb Crissman stumbled into the cage, tripped, went to his hands and knees. He was up instantly, whirling as Starbuck slammed the grille closed and turned the lock.

"Goddamn you!" the outlaw shouted, mouth working convulsively. "I get out of here I'll . . ."

Paying the man no mind, Shawn dropped back to the office. He could hear yelling in the street and other sounds of general confusion as he crossed to the gun rack affixed to the north wall, and glancing through the barred window, he saw Rufus Teague in an excited conversation with Mather and the rest of Cobb Crissman's friends while a small crowd of townspeople listened.

The rack was locked. Looking about for something to pry off the hasp and lock, and finding nothing handy, he picked up the pistol he'd taken from the outlaw chief. Using the barrel of the weapon as a lever, he wedged it under the metal strap and ripped it off.

Grabbing a shotgun and a rifle, he laid both across the desk, placed a box of shells for each alongside after tearing off the covers of the cardboard containers so that their contents would be more readily available.

He could hear Crissman swearing steadily from his cell and grinned faintly as he examined the two weapons he'd set forth to make certain both were loaded. The rifle's magazine was full, but there were no cartridges in the double barrel, and selecting two of the double-ought buckshot shells, he slipped them into the chambers of the weapon.

Crissman continued to rant, cursing and voicing threats at a low shout as Starbuck stepped up close to the window and again threw his glance into the street.

The outlaws and the mayor of Yucca Flat were still talking over the situation. It was apparant that Mather and the other outlaws were preparing to rush the jail, while Teague, with the help of Pete Barkley, was endeavoring to talk them out of it under the watchful eyes of onlooking townspeople. It appeared the mayor had come up with an idea of some sort acceptable to Crissman's friends and that they were going along with it.

Watching them, Starbuck smiled wryly. There was no sign of help for him in sight anywhere along the street; he was in it alone. But that was to be expected. Enforcement of the law was left to men charged with such — and he had assumed that job on his own. While the citizens of a settlement might be all for him and in accord with what he hoped to do, they'd not, for their own safety's sake, raise a finger to help him.

Shawn crowded closer to the dusty glass of the window, turned his gaze to the hotel. From this point along the street it was visible to him. Heather Rustin and the people who'd been on the porch with her were now out in the center of the roadway where they could better see what was taking place in front of the jail. The girl was talking with the drummer and one of the women a little to one side of the others. He hoped Heather would stay where she was; a showdown of some sort was bound to come shortly, and being nearby could be dangerous.

As well bring the issue to a head now, Starbuck decided in that next moment, and picking up the shotgun, he drew back the door of the jail and framed himself in the opening. Instantly a hush fell over the street as, weapon cradled in his arms, he faced the assemblage.

The period of silence held for a long breath, and then a voice demanded, "You trying to get us all killed, mister?"

Shawn swept the crowd with a cool glance as he sought to locate the speaker. It could have been any one of a dozen men glaring at him resentfully. It was not Teague or Pete Barkley, he was certain of that. Both were simply staring at him, surprise still in their eyes.

"No need for anybody to get hurt," he said with a shrug. "Just go on about your business."

Stinger Kenshaw whipped off his hat, dusted it against a knee. "Friend, you're a plain damn fool. How long you figure you can hold out once we make up our minds to come after Cobb?"

"Long enough to put a bullet in his head," Shawn replied calmly. "If you want him alive you'd better forget about rushing me and back

46

off, let things be."

"We ain't never let one of ours lay out in a jail yet — and we ain't about to start now."

"Already started — and he's staying in that cell until after Forsman's executed. By then we'll have a U.S. marshal here and do some looking into what's happened to the deputy. Could be that gallows over there'll have a few more customers."

Kenshaw drew back, glanced at his friends. Mather laughed. "You're a great one for yammering and bamboozling, but you don't scare us none."

"And you're plumb loco if you figure you can hold us off," one of the other outlaws — Jessel, he thought it was — added.

"Can . . . and will," Starbuck said quietly. "Told you before — if you want Crissman to stay alive, keep your distance. First barrel of this scattergun's for whichever one of you's fool enough to make a wrong move; second one's for Crissman. After that, it'll be every man for himself."

"You're missing something, stranger," Job Roanoke drawled. "We don't have to do it that way. Easier to just start taking this here town apart. Like to see how long you'll stand there with that shotgun in your hands when we begin doing that."

"Sure," Stinger Kenshaw said, grinning broadly. "We'll do us a little target practicing, set a fire or two, and maybe grab ourselves a couple of women. . . ."

"Be no need for that!" Rufus Teague shouted apprehensively, raising his hands above his head to forestall such possibilities.

"Reckon there is if we say so," Roanoke snarled. "We ain't no hand at getting horsed around — not when we're holding the top cards."

"You can't blame us for what happened!" Teague shouted. "You know same as us that man's not a part of this town. He's a stranger and just took it on himself to horn in, do what he done."

"Maybe so, but Cobb's locked up there in your jail, and that's a part of your town. Who put him in there don't bale no hay with us — we're just aiming to get him out."

"Leave it to me!" Teague said in a desperate voice as he swiped again at the sweat on his face. "Don't do nothing like what you said — I'll see that Crissman's turned loose."

Roanoke shook his head. "About all we've got from you, old man, is a lot of talking and nothing else."

"You ain't giving me no chance to —"

"We're giving you a chance — right now — about five seconds' worth," Gabe Mather said with a grin.

"Just leave it to me!" Teague pleaded. "Just give me your word you won't start wrecking the town."

"What about Lem?"

"Deal still stands. I'll have him here by sundown."

Mather bobbed his head. "All right, you turn Cobb loose and we'll hold off and just set back and wait like we said we would. Else —"

"Stay right where you are," Teague broke in, relief apparent in his tone and manner as he started toward the jail. "Crissman'll be out here with you in less'n five minutes."

7

Tight-lipped, Starbuck swung the weapon in his hands about, started to level it at the approaching men. And then, with a shrug, he lowered it, stepped back, allowed Teague, Barkley, and a half-dozen others with them to enter the small, stuffy office. When they were all inside, he threw a final, warning glance at the outlaws, motionless in the center of the street, and closed the door.

"Just who the devil you think you are?" Rufus Teague demanded as Shawn turned to face the men. "What right've you got coming in here taking over like you've done?"

Shawn let his eyes drift from one to the other of the group and then settle on the mayor. "Town needs somebody to stand up for the law," he said stiffly.

"So you just up and appoints yourself to do the job high-handed as you please!"

"Had no choice. Nobody else was willing to do it."

Barkley swept off his hat, ran nervous fingers through his hair. "You don't know what you've done! That gang out there in the street's ready to tear this town apart!"

"So they keep telling you. They wouldn't try if

you'd all get together and —"

"Get together against killers like them?" Teague shouted in an exasperated voice. "You're a fool — whoever you are."

"Name's Starbuck," Shawn said, again cradling the shotgun and leaning back against the wall.

From the cell beyond the end of the room Cobb Crissman called, "Better let me out of here! If you don't, mighty quick, you'll all be wishing you'd never seen this day!"

One of the men with Teague crossed hurriedly to where he could see the outlaw. "We're getting you out, Mr. Crissman, right away now."

Shawn spat in disgust. "That all the law means to you people? You've got a killer on your hands that's been sentenced to hang for murdering your own marshal, and you're ready to turn him loose just because a half-dozen show-off hardcases are telling you to."

"If we don't, God only knows what'll happen to the town," Barkley said bitterly. "They've got us between a rock and a hard place. It's the only thing we can do."

"You're wrong!" Starbuck snapped angrily. "You can arm yourselves and tell them to go to hell. . . . I can't understand people like you. The law is something that has to be respected . . . upheld. If it isn't, then we've got nothing."

"That's true — up to a point," Rufus Teague said, calming down somewhat. Pulling out his bandanna, he once again mopped at the sweat blanketing his face. "Sometimes you've got to temper it, make allowances."

"It's justice you temper — not the law."

"That's easy to say, but it ain't always practical to stick to it. What if we do turn Forsman loose? He won't get away for long. Some other town's lawman will throw him in jail for something — maybe another killing — and he'll wind up at the end of a rope just the same."

Shawn stared at the man, finding it hard to believe the words he had heard. "You mean you think it's all right to let a condemned murderer go free on the strength that he'll kill again in some other town and it'll then be up to them to hang him?"

"Time like this, it's the only practical thing to do.

"Not the way I see it," Starbuck said, shaking his head. "This town's got responsibilities to the rest of the country — obligations I guess you could call them —"

"I'm not interested in the rest of the country," Rufus Teague said wearily, "only in my responsibility to the folks living here in Yucca Flat, and that means keeping them from getting hurt and from losing everything they've got. Now, I want you to put that gun down and back off. You stuck your nose into something that's none of your business."

"It is, far as I'm concerned."

"You're dead wrong! And what I'm ordering you to do goes, because I represent the town.

52

What the hell good will it do, anyway, keeping Cobb Crissman locked up?"

"It'll stop that bunch out there in the street from doing any damage, long as he's a hostage — and it'll let the execution of Forsman go through in the morning like the judge ordered."

"What makes you think jugging him will keep them from running wild?"

"That part's up to you. I can hold out here in the jail, and long as he's in a cell, chances are good they won't get out of line, but if they do, a dozen of you men with guns can control them. Be only five against however many you can arm."

"You're talking like a fool," Barkley said. "Nobody's loco enough to think he could fight it out with one of those killers."

"Wouldn't be that way. It'd be several of you against just one of them."

"You're still crazy. You're wanting ordinary men — store owners, clerks, merchants, and the like — to go up against gunfighters, killers who'd as soon shoot you as bat an eye."

"It's the gun that does the killing. A man only has to pull the trigger . . . and he can be hiding behind a door when he does that."

"Makes no difference," Teague said decisively. "I ain't letting this town in for something like that. Bound to get several men killed — all for nothing. Hanging Lem Forsman's not worth it."

"That judge should've had it done somewheres else — a bigger town. Not right, expecting us to do it," Barkley observed.

"Murder took place here," Starbuck said. "Usual for a town to handle its own problems."

"Could've taken him to the capital and —"

"Hey, mayor!" Crissman shouted, rattling the door of his cell. "I'm tired of waiting. You let me out of here or —"

Teague folded his arms across his chest, bucked his head at Shawn. "Turn him loose — right now."

Starbuck did not stir. "It'll be the biggest mistake you'll ever make," he said. "What's to keep them from going back on their word and tearing up your town anyway, once they've got what they want? You think you can trust men like them?"

Rufus Teague's thin shoulders stirred. "I think we've got no other out, that's what. We've got to trust them. Crissman promised he'd give us no trouble if we'd hand over Forsman. Have to take him at his word."

Barkley, glancing through the window, wheeled anxiously to Teague. "That bunch's getting pretty edgy, Rufe. You'd better do something mighty quick."

"Mayor, goddamn you . . ." Crissman's angry voice filled the small office. "Ain't warning you again!"

"Get in there and unlock that cell," Teague said grimly, facing Starbuck. "I'm ordering you to. Maybe you think you're doing the right thing,

54

but you're not. This is different."

"Different!" Shawn echoed scornfully. "You got some idea that yours is the first town that's ever been up against a deal like this? It happens plenty, and most of the time outlaws like Crissman and that gang out there in the street get the worst of it."

"Could be, but I ain't taking the chance. I figure I know what's best for the people that elected me their mayor. . . . Unlock that cell."

Starbuck did not move. "No."

One of the men in the party who had stepped up beside Barkley at the window pivoted abruptly. Light glinted off a pistol in his hand.

"You heard the mayor," he said, cocking the weapon. "Open that door."

Shawn's mouth pulled down into a hard line. "You want to turn him loose, then you do it. I won't."

Rufus Teague swore in exasperation. Crossing to the desk, he snatched up the ring of keys lying upon it, tossed them to Barkley.

"Let him out, Pete. This's gone far enough."

8

Shawn, the double barrel still resting in his folded arms, watched the owner of the general store hurry to the end of the room. A moment later he heard the key grate in the lock of the cage door. The man near the window holstered his pistol and glanced out into the street.

"Ain't none too soon," he said in a low voice. "That bunch looks like they're about to start something."

"No need to worry about them now," Teague said reassuringly. "Crissman'll keep them in hand." He hesitated, attention swinging toward the cell as the outlaw leader, eyes hard and angry, stamped into the room. "Can depend on that, can't we, Cobb?"

Crissman, giving no answer, stalked up to the desk. Picking up his pistol, laid there by Starbuck after he'd used it as a means for opening the gun cabinet, he examined it briefly and slid it into its holster. Raising his gaze, he nodded coldly to Shawn.

"Me and you've got a little settling to do, friend."

Starbuck shifted the weapon in his arms. "Anytime you say."

The outlaw's lips tightened as his eyes nar-

56

rowed. "That's right — I'll say when."

Teague, patches of sweat shining on his face, stirred anxiously. "What I said there a minute ago, Cobb — that you'll keep your word about making your boys behave — you still mean it, don't you?"

Crissman's mouth split into a sardonic smile. "They're growed men. Ain't a hell of a lot I can do if folks start pushing them around."

"But you told me —"

"Know what I told you, and what you said — and you ain't done nothing but waste time ever since. You was going to get Lem, bring him here."

"Aim to do that — only this thing come up. I'm sending a couple of men after him right now, in fact. Was only waiting till we straightened out this thing of you getting put in jail." Teague wheeled to the men who had accompanied him and Barkley into the office and singled out the one who had held his pistol on Starbuck. "Aaron, you and Norm saddle up and ride out to the Taichert place, fetch Lem back here."

Aaron, a squat, middle-aged man with a ruddy complexion, nodded, moved toward the door. Norm, a somewhat younger man with a lean, dark face, stepped in behind him.

"Just don't turn him loose, now," Teague called after them, and then cast an apologetic glance at Crissman. "Want you to bring him here so's I can hand him over to Cobb — prove we're doing what we promised. He just might take a notion to light out once you take the ropes off'n him, leave us holding the bag."

Crissman grinned. "Yeah, you best be sure. . . . Me and the boys'll be waiting at the saloon."

"Fine, fine," Teague said hurriedly. "Just make yourselves to home over there. Drinks'll be on me — on the town. Won't take more'n an hour to get Lem."

"Sundown, that's when your time's up," the outlaw reminded, and then, the smile gone, he glanced coldly at Shawn. "We'll be meeting later."

"Expect we will," Starbuck answered, and watched Crissman pivot, cross to the door, and step out into the open.

Drawing himself away from the wall, Starbuck returned the shotgun to its place in the rack and turned to the window. Crissman was rejoining his friends, all of whom were grinning broadly. Baker, the boyish-looking killer, whipped out his pistol, fired all six cartridges into the air as a noisy salute that set several dogs to barking and started people collected along the street to gravitating toward safer areas.

"Want you to know I'm obligated to you for what you was trying to do, Starbuck."

At the sound of Teague's voice, Shawn came about. "Would've been better if you'd listened to me."

"Maybe seems that way from where you're standing. Truth is, I couldn't do nothing else."

"Can't agree with that, but I'm not going to hash it all over with you again."

58

"Forsman'll get what's coming to him, just like the mayor said," Pete Barkley put in. "Some other town'll trip him up, and he'll swing just the same. Be no difference except it'll happen somewheres besides Yucca Flat."

"No difference — except he'll have killed another man, or maybe this time it'll be a woman," Starbuck said dryly.

Teague shrugged, rubbed at the back of his neck. Another spate of gunshots sounded in the street, this time coming from in front of the Border Queen. The mayor stepped quickly to the door, glanced out, and then smiled weakly.

"Just them cutting up," he said. "Ain't doing no damage."

"They've done a plenty of that already," one of the remaining men who had followed Teague and Barkley into the office at the beginning observed doubtfully. "I ain't so sure now we did the right thing."

"No choice," Teague said again wearily. "Don't go worrying about it."

"Well, I'm hoping it's about over with," Barkley said. "Had all I can take — almost."

"It's a long way from being over," Starbuck said as the men moved toward the door. "Better make up your minds to that."

Teague paused, looked back over a shoulder, clearly irritated. "You riding on?"

"Figured to stay the night."

"I'd as soon you'd pull out now, but I reckon it is a mite late. Be obliged to you if you'll be gone by morning — and keep out of sight till then."

Shawn smiled, made no reply as he watched the men pass through the doorway and out into the now quiet, deserted street. Crissman and his followers were no longer in evidence, apparently having gone inside the Border Queen, where they were beginning to enjoy the hospitality of the town as set forth by Mayor Teague. In another hour or so — by sunset — they would be in a mood that could spell far more problems for Yucca Flat than Rufus Teague could imagine.

Shawn had done what he could to prevent such from coming to pass, but his efforts had gone for nothing. The leaders of the settlement — at least the majority of them — had deemed it wiser to pacify trouble than stop it cold; and, alone, a stranger among them, his word had carried no weight. Thus he could do no more; best he simply forget it, mark it down as another time the law had gone begging for want of a champion.

Drawing himself up, Starbuck moved toward the exit to return to the hotel, where Heather Rustin would be awaiting him. The thud of boot heels outside the jail brought him to a halt.

Shortly Ross Sargent stepped into view, and crossing the landing, entered the heat-filled room. With him were two men, one a tall, raw-boned blond with wide, powerful shoulders and a long, ruddy face; the other was of average height but heavily built and wore a baggy gray suit, white shirt, and bow tie. Except for a small, pointed goatee, he was clean-shaven. Sargent, somewhat ill-at-ease, halted in front of the desk. Nodding to Shawn, he pointed to the tall man.

"Starbuck, like you to shake hands with Asa Jorgenson. Runs the feed store across the street."

Shawn extended his hand, took that of Jorgenson's in his, and glanced to the man beside him.

"This here's Doc Schultz," the livery stable owner continued.

The introductions completed, Starbuck resumed his position of shoulders against the wall and folded his arms across his chest. The three had something on their minds, that was certain; if it was an offer to help — to stand with him against Teague and Barkley — they had come a bit late.

"We've been talking," Sargent said. "I told them how you felt about the way the town was dodging its responsibilities, and we all agree with you. Like I said earlier, I got outvoted by the other members of the council when it came to turning down Crissman — me and Mason Ryder."

"Where is Ryder?" Schultz asked in a faintly accented voice. "He ought to be here."

"Figured he'd be in for plenty of trouble, what with Rufus the same as telling that bunch they could take over his saloon, so he's sticking close. Can count on him, however, to string along with whatever we decide to do."

"And what's that to be?" Shawn asked quietly,

his coolness apparent.

Sargent cleared his throat, rubbed at a jaw uncertainly. "Well, we don't exactly know. Thought maybe you'd have an idea."

Starbuck smiled wryly. "Too late for the one I had. Little late for most everything."

Schultz nodded. "Wolves are already loose in the fold, for a fact. It is too bad we could not get together sooner."

Jorgenson reached into the pocket of his shirt, produced a plug of tobacco, and bit off a corner.

"It's honest I will be with you, Starbuck," he said, his tones also slightly foreign. "I thought, like Rufe, we could maybe get rid of those bad ones by going along with what they wanted. I was wrong. A man cannot take a serpent unto his bosom and not become its victim."

"And we've got to stand up for what's right, no matter what it costs," Sargent continued. "Reckon we all see that now, but like you say, it's a little late, but we're wondering if there ain't something we can do."

Shawn considered the men in silence. Loud talking and laughing were coming from the Border Queen, and he reckoned Cobb Crissman and his bunch were enjoying themselves to the fullest. They were now the problem of Mason Ryder, the owner of the saloon, as far as Teague, Barkley, and whoever else it was that had voted to give in to the outlaws were concerned. They were busily and safely occupied elsewhere in

Yucca Flat, and it was up to him to cope with them.

"Could be there is," Starbuck said finally.

Interest broke quickly in the eyes of the three men. Sargent smiled tautly. "Whatever you're thinking, spit it out."

"It'll maybe come down to using a gun. . . ."

"Expected that," Sargent said.

Schultz's thick shoulders lifted, fell. "I am not so good at that, but I am willing to do my part."

"I have a shotgun," Jorgenson said. "It is old, but it works good."

"Plenty of rifles right here," Shawn said, jerking a thumb at the rack on the wall. "Chance you won't need to use a gun anyway — only make a show of strength. Important thing to me is that I've got to know for sure I'll have some backing if I go ahead with what I'm thinking."

"Can figure on us, and Ryder. Pretty sure we can hustle up a couple or three more men. Way that bunch was acting out there changed a few minds, I'm pretty sure."

Starbuck nodded. There was little doubt that many of the townspeople would be regretting the course Rufus Teague and the majority of the council had followed, but it likely would end there; they would take no positive steps to correct the situation.

"What do you want us to do?" Schultz asked, moving to the window.

"Nothing for now — and the less you know about what I'm planning, the better. Want this to look to Crissman like it's all my doing, that nobody else in town had any part of it."

"Then why . . ." Sargent began, puzzled.

"Where you'll come in will be later — and maybe not even then if things don't work out right. Point is, I need to know there are a few people I can depend on."

Doc Schultz nodded. "I see. You are arranging this so that Cobb Crissman will blame you for whatever is done, and not the town."

"About the way of it. Reason why it's just as well you don't know what I'm up to."

"Don't seem right, you taking this on yourself like you are," Sargent said.

"Better an outsider than somebody that's part of the town. Earlier, while we had Crissman locked up, it would have been different, but that's all changed now. . . . Another thing, best you don't let on that we've had this talk."

"No problem there," the medical man said, again glancing into the street. "Everybody's taken cover. Doubt if anyone knows we're in here."

"Good, let's keep it that way. When I leave, I'll go out the back. You stall for a few minutes, then do the same. If anybody's watching, they won't be watching the back door. . . . Need to know one thing. . . ."

The three men faced Shawn. Sargent said, "What's that?"

"Place where they've got Forsman holed up; where is it?"

"Taichert's," the livery stable owner said. "It's a homestead ten, twelve miles from here — just this side of the hills. Deserted. Taichert pulled out years ago. Can't miss it if you take the road heading west at the end of the street."

Starbuck nodded, signifying his understanding, and opening the top drawer of the desk, began to rummage about in it. Not finding what he sought, he closed it, pulled out the second compartment, grunted in satisfaction. Besides a pistol and several boxes of ammunition, there was a pair of handcuffs. Taking them out, he tried the key, made certain the chain-linked bands were in working order. Satisfied, he slipped them into a pocket, and bucking his head at the three men, started for the rear of the jail. Jorgenson's voice followed him.

"You going out to get Lem?"

Shawn did not pause, merely glanced over his shoulder and smiled.

"See you all later," he said.

9

Gaining the alley behind the jail and other buildings along that side of the street, Starbuck backtracked to the hotel. As he rounded the corner of the structure and stepped up onto the porch, he had a fleeting glimpse of the two men, Aaron and Norm, that Rufus Teague had dispatched to get Lem Forsman. Leading a spare horse, they were just topping a low rise to the west.

"Shawn . . ."

Heather's voice, filled with relief and welcome, came to him as he stepped through the doorway of the hostelry and entered the lobby. He grinned, glanced about. The drummer, deep in a barrel chair near a window, was leafing through a magazine. There was no one else present.

"Are you all right?" the girl asked anxiously. "I saw you out there in the street . . . with those outlaws. And then someone said the mayor had made you —"

"Everything's fine," Shawn cut in, silencing her flow of words. "You get yourself settled?"

"No, I was waiting for you to come . . ."

"I see. Want you to rent a room, stay inside the hotel."

"Is there going to be trouble?"

66

The drummer carefully lowered his magazine, leaned forward so that he might hear better.

"Possible. Best you not go out on the street. I'll be gone for a spell."

A worried frown puckered the girl's brow, but she shook it off almost immediately, as if she knew there was no need for anxiety where he was concerned.

"All right. When will you be back?"

"Maybe tonight — morning for sure," Starbuck said, glancing around. His eyes halted on the entrance to the restaurant at the end of the lobby. "Take your meals in there. I'll settle up with the clerk tomorrow. And have him take care of your horse. They've got a barn out back, I noticed."

Heather nodded slowly. "Can't you tell me where you're going?"

"Best you don't know," he replied, smiling, and touching the brim of his hat with a forefinger, wheeled and returned to the porch.

The street was still deserted, and the racket within the Border Queen was a steady din, he noted as he crossed to the hitch rack and swung onto the sorrel. With luck it would develop into nothing more serious than just noise.

Cutting sharply about, Starbuck rode along the alley until he found a path that angled off to the west. Heading the gelding onto it, he kept the big horse to a brisk walk. The well-beaten trail, used apparently by occupants of several houses standing back from the town as a route to and from the stores, shortly broke away from the small structures and merged with the clearly defined road that continued on westward.

At once Starbuck roweled the gelding into a lope, swung him onto the softer shoulder of the roadway, where the drum of the horse's hoofs would be deadened. Aaron and Norm could not be far ahead; in fact, he should have them in sight within only minutes. If that proved to be true, he would save himself time that otherwise might be spent in looking for homesteader Taichert's abandoned property.

The place was nearer the settlement than he expected. Following the road across a flat toward a line of fairly high hills, Shawn broke suddenly down into a deep broad wash. Gaining its opposite side and climbing a short slope, he found himself on a narrow mesa that butted against a row of bluffs. Huddled at the base of their ragged facades was a small weather-worn shack. Three horses waited close by.

Satisfaction stirred through Starbuck. It was working out better than he'd hoped. The two men, taking advantage of the ample time remaining until sundown, were not pressing themselves.

Staying clear of the road, Shawn dropped back, and swinging wide of the sagging house, came up to it from its lower side. A safe distance below, he halted in a stand of cedars and buckbrush. Dismounting, he tied the sorrel to one of the squat little trees and made his way quietly to the shack. Aaron's voice came to him as he paused just outside the open door.

"Job's mine. Teague same as told me so after the deputy turned up missing."

"Should've pinned that star on you right then," a second voice, undoubtedly that of Norm, declared. "If he had, the town'd have a lawman now instead —"

"Come on, come on — cut out the jawing and get these damn ropes off'n me!"

The third man would be Lem Forsman, impatient to be released from his bonds. Shawn drew his pistol, checked the loads.

"I get the marshal's job, I'll be needing a good deputy," Aaron continued. "You stick by me through this, back me all the way, and the badge is yours."

"Don't worry, that's just what I'll be doing. . . . We have to keep Lem tied up going back to town?"

"Reckon we'd best. You recollect what Teague said —"

"What the hell for?" Lem Forsman cut in angrily. "I'm getting turned loose, ain't I?"

"Yeah, sure, but the mayor sort of wants to hand you over to Crissman personal like. Make a show of it. We won't do nothing except keep your hands tied. That jake with you?"

The outlaw grumbled something in reply to Aaron and then added, "Took Cobb long enough to show up. Few things I aim to say to him when we meet up — letting me lay around in that goddamned jail all them days like he done."

"Well, you're out now," Aaron said; and then, with brisk authority: "Let's go."

Forsman laughed. "Hell, you're already talking like a marshal!"

"Just what I'll be when this is all over."

"Well, don't go trying it out on me," the outlaw said. "Tin stars come a penny a dozen, far as I'm concerned."

Starbuck drew back from the doorway. Gun in hand, he plastered himself against the wall. The scuffing and thudding of boots on the hard clay floor of the shadow-filled shack reached him. Abruptly Aaron appeared in the entrance. He paused briefly, stepped into the open, Norm following at his heels.

Shawn gathered his muscles, lunged, drove a shoulder into the latter. The deputy-to-be yelled, crashed into Aaron. The two went down in a tangle of legs and arms, both cursing wildly.

From inside the hut came Forsman's startled voice. "What the hell's going on?"

"Stay in there," Starbuck ordered, and moving forward, bent over the struggling men and relieved them of their weapons. Stepping back, he watched them scramble to their feet.

"You!" Aaron snarled, anger flushing his dust-covered features. "Might've knowed it'd be you horning in! If I had my gun —"

"Ease off," Starbuck said coolly. "I've got nothing against you or your friend there, so don't force my hand."

70

Aaron brushed at his face, spat the dirt from his mouth that he'd accumulated while on the ground. "What the hell's this all about?"

"I'm taking Forsman."

Aaron straightened, cast a side glance at Norm. "Ain't nobody taking a prisoner from me!"

Shawn shook his head, smiled. "Don't try being a hero — you'll never make it, neither one of you."

"You know what this is going to mean to the town?" Aaron asked after a long pause, taking a different tack. "Crissman and them'll tree —"

"They won't do any more to it than they've already done, long as you listen to what I tell you."

"What's that?"

"Head back, tell Crissman I'll turn Forsman over to him in the morning. It's a personal deal, between him and me, and the town's got nothing to do with it. Want you to make that clear to Crissman."

"Something between you and him, or between you and Lem?"

"Crissman. Forsman's just my ace-in-the-hole."

Aaron again spat. "Why don't you do it now? Why're you holding off?"

"Some things need straightening out first," Starbuck answered, sidestepping the question. "You just do what I tell you."

A slyness came into Aaron's eyes. He glanced

71

again at Norm. "All right, mister, you're calling the shots. You going to lay out here for the night."

"Maybe. . . . Now, head out. Want Crissman to get my message in plenty of time," Shawn said as he thumbed open the loading gate of the pistols he'd taken from the two men and dropped the cartridges into the dust.

"Tell him I said to keep this strictly between him and me, that if he gives the town any trouble, I won't show up with Forsman. Instead, I'll lay out along the road and bushwhack him and his bunch one by one when they ride on."

Aaron caught the empty weapon tossed to him by Starbuck, dropped it into his holster.

"This some kind of a grudge you got going with him? That what this's all about?"

"Reckon you could say that. He can look for me right after sunrise."

"Where? Anyplace special?"

"Porch of the hotel will do."

Aaron nodded, turned toward his horse. Norm, still holding the empty weapon returned to him at his side, wheeled, followed.

"I'll be keeping an eye on you," Shawn warned, guessing at what would be in the minds of the two men. "Try any tricks, and neither one of you'll live to pin on those stars you're hoping to get!"

"Why, we ain't —"

"Means leaving those guns unloaded and forgetting about doubling back. Where I'm taking

Forsman, it'll be easy to watch for you."

"We won't be trying nothing," Aaron said resignedly as they moved off.

"That's the way to play it smart as well as stay healthy. . . . Can prove you're a good lawman, too, by making Cobb Crissman understand he'd better not hooraw the town any over this."

Aaron slowed his horse, shrugged. "Can sure try, but I ain't for certain he'll listen."

"Point I'm bringing out. You've got to make him listen. It's for the sake of the town — your town."

"Yeah, can see what you mean. . . . What'll I tell the mayor? He's figuring on —"

"Can say I took Forsman off his hands, that he don't need to worry about him anymore."

"Sure ain't going to set good with him," Aaron said with a gusty sigh. "But, way I see it, he ain't got no choice."

"Expect that covers it."

"Wouldn't be no call for none of this if you and Crissman'd settle your grudge somewheres else," Norm observed sourly, finally getting into the conversation.

"Time and place don't count," Starbuck said. "Chance comes to prove something that's important to him, a man best grab it. . . . Ride on. I don't want you to be late."

10

For a time Starbuck did not stir, his attention on the two men moving off across the flat; and then, when they dropped from sight, he turned to the shack.

"Come on out, Forsman."

There was the quiet sound of the outlaw's stealthy steps, and finally his voice. "Hell with you. You want me . . . come in here after me."

Starbuck swore impatiently. He wanted to get away from the Taichert place as quickly as possible in the event Norm and Aaron did have a change of mind and decided to circle and make a try at recovering their prisoner. But entering the shack, almost completely black inside now as the sun dropped lower beyond the hills in the west, was the last thing he intended to do.

Forsman's hands were tied, he was certain of that, but the odds were they were linked in front of the outlaw and not behind his back, so as to make riding easier. Thus, wielding a club effectively would be no chore for him, and at that very moment he was likely standing in the deep shadows just inside the doorway awaiting that opportunity.

"Have it your way," Shawn said.

Turning on a heel, he tore a section of dead

branches from a nearby clump of snakeweed. Striking a match to the tinder-dry bit of brush, he waited until it was burning strongly, and then, crossing to the doorway, tossed the crackling, smoking torch into the hut.

Immediately he could hear Forsman tramping about feverishly. Shortly, cursing and choking as the pungent smoke began to pour out of the entrance to the hut, the outlaw appeared.

He was a small, wiry man clad in worn army pants, scarred boots, faded checked shirt, and a wide-brimmed, fairly new hat. He had red hair and a thick black moustache, and his eyes, watering freely from the sharp fumes and smoke of the burning weed clump, appeared to be brown. Gagging, he faced Starbuck.

"Who the hell are you — and what're you wanting me for?"

"Aim to see you keep that date with the hangman in the morning," Shawn replied.

Forsman stared, dug at his smarting eyes with his knuckles. His hands were bound in front of him, as Starbuck had expected.

"You a lawman?"

"No. . . . Get on your horse. We're pulling out."

Forsman did not move. Starbuck flung a glance toward the road. There was no sign of riders, but if Aaron and Norm were doubling back, they would not be thoughtless enough to let themselves be seen; they would, instead, be keeping to the brush and cedars. Reaching out, he put a hand against Forsman's shoulder, pushed him roughly toward his waiting horse.

"You can ride sitting on the saddle, or slung across it," he said. "Up to you."

The outlaw stumbled, caught himself, and halted beside the bay horse brought for his use. Gripping the horn with both hands, he heaved himself aboard. Shawn waited until the man had found the stirrups, and then, taking the bay's reins, led him to where he'd left the sorrel.

Climbing onto his mount, Starbuck gripped the ends of the bay's leathers in his hand and started the sorrel on the trail that cut up through the bluffs south of Taichert's. He'd have to lead Forsman's horse; his rope had been lost somewhere in Mexico, and there was none hanging from the outlaw's saddle. The short reins kept the bay uncomfortably close to the heels of the sorrel, but for the time being there was no other alternative.

"Where we heading?" Forsman demanded peevishly.

"High country," Starbuck replied, nodding toward the slopes of the hills lying beyond the bluffs.

"What for? Hell, we could've stayed there in that shack. . . . What're you cutting yourself in on this shindig for, anyway, if you ain't no lawman?"

Shawn, as the horses pulled up onto the crest of the rocky formations, again looked off to the flat. There was still no indication of Norm or

76

Aaron. He guessed they had taken him at his word and were hurrying on to Yucca Flat.

"Not right, you using me to get back at Cobb Crissman — just because you and him've got a grudge."

"You've got no rights, Forsman," Starbuck said indifferently. "You're a murderer, and you've been sentenced to hang. Your claim to having rights ended there — when you shot that marshal in the back — so don't push me. Nothing says I have to keep you alive."

Putting a bullet in the outlaw was the last thing Starbuck wanted to do; the sentence pronounced by the judge had to be carried out as scheduled if anything was to be gained and the law strengthened. But that was something Lem Forsman didn't need to know at that moment; he would be easier controlled throughout the long night that lay ahead if he believed he might get himself shot should he make any attempt to escape.

They pressed on, climbing steadily and now entering an area of heavier growth — oaks, junipers, a few pines — on the slope that lifted up from the buttes. Shawn had no intention of getting too far from the settlement, only wanted to find a higher, safer location well away from the Taichert homestead where he could leave his prisoner.

It should not be a difficult choice; around them he noted dense patches of scrub oak, mountain mahogany, and similar brush standing among the trees, and there were large boulders strewn across the grade, creating bulwarks which could keep a man from being seen from the country below.

Somewhere off to their left a coyote yipped into the closing darkness, evoking an answer from the foothills to the south. The moon was already out, only a pale crescent well up in the sky, promising but little light for the coming night.

"When are we stopping?" Forsman grumbled. "Ain't easy riding this way . . . and them damned stirrups are too long."

Starbuck shrugged, but he reckoned they were far enough from Taichert's to halt, and glancing about, selected a large rock wedged against two towering pines as a suitable campsite and made for it. Not only would the combination of the trees and rock provide excellent cover, but it would be easily found when he returned from the settlement. Pulling into the fan of deep shadows, he halted, and dropping the reins of Forsman's bay, swung down.

Instantly Starbuck knew he had made a mistake. The quick squeak of leather warned him. He jerked to one side as Forsman launched himself from the saddle. The outlaw's outstretched hands clawed for Shawn's shoulders, missed, and the man hit the ground on all fours with a solid thud.

He was up and wheeling in only a fraction of time. Starbuck, off balance, pivoted unsteadily.

Hands locked into a double fist, the outlaw clubbed him high on the head. Shawn, unhurt, rocked, and measuring Forsman coolly, dropped him to his knees with a shocking right to the jaw.

Breathing hard from the unexpected effort, Starbuck stepped back. Reaching into his pocket, he obtained the cuffs he'd taken from the desk drawer in the jail, and then, drawing his knife from its boot sheath, cut the rope that linked the outlaw's wrists. That done, he dragged the stunned Forsman to the nearest of the two pines, turned him about so that his back was against its trunk, and pulling his arms to the opposite side, affixed the metal cuffs. It was an uncomfortable position, one that could become painful if the outlaw struggled against the steel restraints.

Forsman, conscious again, glared at Starbuck in the pale light. "I'll get loose yet," he snarled. "You'll see. And when I do . . ."

Starbuck smiled faintly, and taking the bandanna hanging from the outlaw's pocket, he twisted it into a loose cord and tied it securely across the man's mouth. Forsman jerked his head from side to side in an effort to escape the gag, but to no avail.

Shawn moved then to the bay, led him off into a close-by thicket, and tethered him with the reins. Thin grass covered the open patches of ground between the brush, and the horse immediately began to graze. Contented, he would not

79

stray far, even if he succeeded in jerking the leather straps free.

Darkness was complete when Starbuck had completed that chore and had returned to where he'd left Lem Forsman and his own horse. The coyote was voicing his complaints again into the night as he hunched beside the outlaw, raving unintelligibly behind the bandanna gag, to make a final check of the handcuffs and the gag. Finding them both to his satisfaction, he rose, crossed to the sorrel.

"I'm taking a ride into town, see how things are going," he said as he went onto the saddle.

Forsman strained against the pine, gave it up quickly as pain wrenched his shoulders. Settling back, he glared at Starbuck over the top of the gag while he continued to mutter incomprehensible oaths and threats.

"I'll bring back some grub," Shawn said, and then added: "Maybe a bottle of whiskey for you."

Cutting the sorrel about, he rode out from behind the rock and headed down the slope. Outlaw or not, a man about to die was entitled to a little consideration, he supposed.

11

The night was pleasantly cool, and as the sorrel gelding loped easily along, cutting through the sandy arroyos and across the grassy flats where the pale, meager light turned the clumps of Apache plume into mounds of shredded silver and silhouetted the gaunt chollas, Starbuck considered what yet had to be done.

He had succeeded in preventing Lem Forsman from escaping the penalty assessed by the law — so far. The final act was still to come, and it would be the most difficult of all to fulfill.

Much depended upon timing, but most of all those few members of the town who professed a desire to see justice done must perform the tasks he would require of them. Ross Sargent, Doc Schultz, Asa Jorgenson, and, hopefully, Mason Ryder, the owner of the Border Queen Saloon — each would have to do his part. If, at the last moment, they faltered, shrank from their duties, Shawn knew he would find himself in a desperate situation, one he most likely would not survive.

He grinned wryly as he topped the last rise and looked down on the scattered lights of the settlement. Why had he let himself get involved — again — in someone else's problem? Why

81

couldn't he have just gone on about the business of finding his brother? Hell, he hadn't even taken time to make inquiries as to whether Ben was in Yucca Flat or not!

But it was a bit late to think about that now, and he could not have, in all conscience, stood by and allowed Cobb Crissman and his outlaws to have their way. It would all be over and done with shortly after sunrise that next morning, anyway, and he could then resume the search for Ben — assuming he was still alive.

Shawn shrugged off that grim thought, and reaching the first of the town's outlying residences, swung in between them, and to the accompaniment of several disturbed dogs that appeared to do their barking in relays, followed a course that brought him to the rear of the hotel.

Pulling up in the dark shadows, Starbuck dismounted, and tying the gelding to a post, walked quietly along the wall of the structure to the front for a look at the street.

Only a few lamps were alight, and the yellow glow fanning out from them lent the dusty, silent roadway a mysterious, almost eerie effect. The stores that had borne the brunt of the Crissman gang's horseplay were in total darkness, most with sheets of canvas stretched over their gaping, shattered windows.

There was no one in sight along the sidewalks, which ordinarily at that cool hour would have seen considerable traffic, since it was the ideal time for shopping. But now a pall lay over the settlement, and the residents were keeping indoors hoping to stay out of harm's way.

The Border Queen, while well lighted, was curiously quiet. Crissman and his bunch were still inside, Shawn reckoned, and apparently, heeding the warning he'd given Aaron for them, were restraining themselves — most likely from curiosity and not fear. Men of such caliber did not frighten easily.

Starbuck moved up onto the hotel's gallery. The scattering of chairs upon it was empty, and crossing to the door again, he halted. The lobby was dim, lit by only two wall lamps that had been turned low. He could see no one present, and drawing back the dust-clogged screen, he stepped inside and drew up before the desk. The hangman's name was Leviticus, Ross Sargent had said. It was necessary that he find the man, have a talk with him.

There was no one in the chair behind the desk. Starbuck turned his attention to the board from which several keys with numbered tags were hanging. There were a half-dozen empty hooks, which could only mean the hotel was enjoying the patronage of that many guests; only one would be Leviticus.

"Evenin' . . ."

Starbuck came about slowly, a jolt of disappointment coursing through him. It was important that he not be seen, particularly by Crissman or any of his friends. It was the drummer, smiling broadly, a big cigar between the fingers of his left hand.

"It's a quiet one," Shawn murmured, wondering how much the traveling man knew of the situation.

"Not hard to understand. Everybody — including me — is scared to go out, way things are. . . . You looking for your wom . . . for the lady who's with you?"

Shawn nodded. "Forgot to ask which room she's in."

"Number three — right between me and the hangman," the drummer replied. "Like to buy you a drink — sort of celebrate whatever it is you're trying to do. There's a bar right here in the hotel's restaurant."

"Obliged to you, but I'm a bit pressed for time," Starbuck said.

The drummer shrugged indifferently, expelled a cloud of smoke, and turning, retreated for the room separated from the lobby by heavy portieres from which he'd evidently come.

"I'll ask a favor of you," Starbuck called quietly after the man.

The drummer paused. "Yeah?"

"You haven't seen me. Best for everybody's sake."

"Sure, won't mention it to a soul," the salesman replied, and shouldered his way on through the curtains.

Word reaching Crissman that he was in town was the last thing Starbuck wanted at that moment, for to have the outlaws confront him now would void all his carefully laid plans. He hoped he could rely on the drummer to live up to his word.

Moving into the hallway that he could see beyond the desk, Shawn proceeded down it until he came to the door bearing the number three. Knocking softly, he waited. Leviticus would be in either room two or four, and Heather could tell him which.

The varnished, scarred panel swung back, and the girl stood framed in its opening, outlined by the lamplight coming from behind her. She was still wearing the clothing she had worn on the trail, but she had managed to brush out her hair, and it now hung about her head in a soft halo.

"Shawn!" she cried softly, a smile of relief and welcome parting her lips. "I was hoping —"

"Wasn't sure I'd see you until morning," he said, stepping into the room and closing the door.

She drew back anxiously. "Is everything all right? I heard you'd taken that man — that killer — they were going to hang away from the —"

"Everything's fine," he broke in gently, hoping to ease her anxiety. "Don't worry about it. . . . What I need to know is which room a man named Leviticus is in. He's the one that was sent here to hang Forsman."

Heather frowned, sat down on the edge of the bed. "Leviticus? I don't know. I haven't —"

"Was talking to that drummer, the one we saw

on the porch. Said he was next to you. Which side?"

The girl smiled. "Oh, yes, Mr. Bixby. He was at the supper table tonight with me and some other folks. He's in number two."

That meant the hangman would be in number four. Starbuck nodded, and suddenly remembering, reached into a pocket for a gold eagle. Handing it to Heather, he turned to the door.

"Use this for whatever you want. I'll be back in the morning."

"But, Shawn . . . wait," the girl began, and fell silent. He was already in the hallway and pulling the panel shut behind him.

Starbuck stepped hurriedly to the adjacent door, rapped quietly on the thin wood.

A chair scraped somewhere inside the room, and then a voice inquired at low pitch. "Yes?"

"Open up," Shawn answered, glancing toward the lobby. He was still having doubts as to the drummer. "Need to talk to you."

A key grated, and the door swung in. A small, gray man with the subdued mien of a mortician peered out at Starbuck through steel-rimmed spectacles.

"What is it you want?"

Shawn pushed roughly by the man into the room and closed the door.

"You're John Leviticus?"

"I am," the man replied, faintly angered. "Who're you?"

"Name's Starbuck. I've taken charge of the

execution you're to handle in the morning."

Leviticus frowned, ran a finger inside the closed neckband of his collarless shirt. "I . . . I don't understand. Was told the execution had been called off. . . . I aimed to catch the stage —"

"It's to go through like it was planned. Reason I dropped by to see you, make sure you knew that. I'll have Lem Forsman at the gallows by sunrise in the morning. Want you there ready to do your job."

"I see," Leviticus said. "You the new lawman here?"

"No."

"Where from, then? Know you're not the U.S. marshal. I'm acquainted with him."

"Guess you can say I just volunteered for the marshal's job — until this is over with."

A tightness came into the hangman's eyes. "What about those friends of Forsman's? From what I've been told, they're liable to object, try to stop it."

"I'll see to them. You won't be interfered with. Everything understood?"

"Guess it is. Execution is to take place at sunup in the morning, just as the judge ordered."

"That's it. . . . One thing more. You're to keep this quiet, not mention it to anybody. Gawkers will only get in the way, and since people around here think the hanging's been called off, we'll let them continue to believe that."

"But we'll have to have witnesses. The law requires that —"

"I'll arrange for them. Be a doctor there, too, so's the death can be certified."

"That's not exactly necessary, but it is a good idea. Is there anything else?"

"Only one thing. When you head for the gallows in the morning, use the back door of the hotel and walk down the alley."

John Leviticus swallowed noisily, and the tightness came into his eyes again. "If there's going to be trouble, I'd as soon —"

"Be no danger to you as long as you do what I've told you. It's just that we're having to go about this in a little different way. . . . Now, if you'd feel better, I can take you up to the jail, lock you in a cell. You'd be plenty safe, because nobody'd think to look for you there."

Leviticus mustered a small smile. "No, I'll stay here in my room — and I'll be there on time in the morning. This is nothing new on my job. A man about to be hanged always has a few friends."

"Guess we're all set, then," Starbuck said, and reached for the knob. "See you at sunrise. . . . Good night."

He heard Leviticus make his response as he stepped out into the hall and turned for the lobby. Immediately, loud voices coming from that area brought him to a sudden halt. It was some of Crissman's bunch — perhaps all of them.

Shawn dropped back to the opposite end of the narrow corridor where he could see the dim

88

outlines of a door, one leading to the outside, he assumed. He drew up sharply, a curse slipping from his lips. The door was secured by a hasp and padlock.

12

Heather Rustin sank back onto the bed, all the bright spirit and bubbling happiness that had filled her at sight of Shawn draining swiftly. She'd had so much to tell him, such good news — but there'd been no time.

It was those outlaws, that murderer who was supposed to be hanged, that occupied his mind and was shutting her out. Why did he have to take a hand in the affair? Why couldn't he have just let things be? Heather sighed resignedly. He was gone, but no great harm done; he'd be back, and she guessed she'd better start getting used to a man like Shawn, who, she'd learned since meeting him in Mexico, never deviated from a course, once undertaken. She'd tell him all about their future when she saw him in the morning.

It had all started while they were standing on the hotel's porch watching Mr. Teague, the mayor, try to come to some agreement with the outlaws. Shawn had gone on for a closer look and then had taken a hand in the argument, which hadn't set very well with the mayor, Mrs. Teague had said later. But the fact that he had and was planning to do more had impressed Mrs. Teague nevertheless, as well as the others.

90

The mayor's wife; the elderly couple, Mr. and Mrs. Luckett — he was a retired rancher and apparently well off financially; Mrs. Kovacks, the widow of one of the town's early settlers; Mr. Hatfield, a cattle buyer from up in Kansas somewhere; and Mr. Bixby, the drummer, had all listened, deeply interested while she told them about Shawn.

Only Mr. Hatfield had taken her accounting lightly, seemingly thinking what he had done down in Mexico was of little consequence, and remarked that Shawn would probably end up like the rest of the men in town, letting the outlaws have their way. But what Mr. Hatfield thought didn't amount to a row of peas. He didn't even live in Yucca Flat and had no right to say anything. Besides, he'd be gone in another day or two.

Mr. Luckett was something else. He had a lot of influence around the town, was even considering going into politics. Mrs. Kovacks, too, having lived there since the settlement began, had many friends who'd listen to her. And of course Mrs. Teague's word would carry a lot of weight with her husband.

It was strange how it all worked out. She had become friendly with all of them while they were there on the gallery, and then later, after she'd engaged a room, cleaned up as best she could since she had no change of clothes, she'd gone to the restaurant, which was just off the hotel's lobby.

91

The Lucketts were already there at one of the tables, and he had risen and beckoned to her.

"Why not take your meal with us, Mrs. Rustin?" he'd said.

She'd felt a bit lonely without Shawn after all those days and nights of constant association, and had accepted gladly. Scarcely had she sat down when Mr. Bixby came in, and Luckett had called him over, too. They were just glancing at the bill of fare when Mrs. Kovacks appeared, and dragging up another chair, Mr. Luckett had brought her into the party also.

"We're getting to be like a family," the widow had said. "It's all very pleasant."

"Except for what's going on out there in the street," the drummer commented.

"Don't worry, that will all be taken care of," Heather replied confidently. "Shawn is as good as any marshal — better than most, I suspect."

"Well, the job's open," Bixby said with a smile. "Why don't he apply for it?"

"Now, that's a thought," Mr. Luckett said, leaning forward. "With Arlie Pringle and Dave Gallinger gone — dead — the town will need a good man."

"He's not going to be very popular with Teague," Bixby said. "Way I heard it, he just sort of took the play out of the mayor's hands and started running things himself."

"That's what we need, a man who's not afraid to make a decision — not that Rufus Teague hasn't done a mighty fine job as mayor. I'm talking about a lawman."

"Rufus has been a good mayor," Mrs. Kovacks agreed, fingering the lace collar of her black dress.

"But he needs a strong hand in the marshal's office," Luckett continued. "We can't expect him to do everything, and if Mr. Rustin —"

"Starbuck," Heather corrected.

Luckett nodded slightly. "Ah, yes, Starbuck. I got a bit mixed up."

"She said they were going to get married, probably right here in Yucca Flat," Mrs. Luckett reminded him. "Was no place down there in that . . . that Mexico where the ceremony could be performed. . . . Wouldn't have been legal, anyway — probably."

"We just happened to meet down there, as I said before," Heather said. "I was on my way to Arizona with my husband. We were going to find jobs teaching school, but he was killed."

"You're a teacher?" Luckett asked, his brows arching.

"Why, yes. I taught grades up as high as the tenth back in my home — Cincinnati."

"All this sounds better as we go along," Luckett said, smiling expansively, and then settled back as the waitress came up to take their orders.

When the woman had turned away for the kitchen, Mr. Luckett nodded to his wife and Mrs. Kovacks.

"I have a feeling Mrs. Rustin and her friend

are heaven-sent! At the meeting of the school board only last week the fellow we have teaching told us he wanted to resign and that he'd like for us to find a replacement as soon as possible. Mrs. Rustin, here, can step right in and take over."

"And her husband-to-be can take the job as our town marshal," Mrs. Kovacks finished, smiling happily. "What a nice thing for all of us!"

Bixby placed his hands together, steepled his fingers. "Only one hitch to all that. You're going to have to sell the mayor on the idea, and I've got a feeling he ain't about to go for it."

"Don't you worry about him," Mrs. Luckett said. "I'll talk to Ida Teague. She'll see right away what a good arrangement it'll be. She won't have any trouble convincing Rufus."

"If you need any help, just you let me know," Mrs. Kovacks put in, nodding briskly. "I think it would be a shame if we missed out on getting Mrs. Rustin for our teacher — a terrible shame. It's not often we'd get the chance to hire on someone from one of the big eastern cities."

The drummer laughed. "No, I suppose not, but you can hardly call Cincinnati an eastern city — or a big one, either."

"Maybe not," Mrs. Kovacks said stiffly, "but you all know what I mean."

"Men with the qualities of this fellow Starbuck don't come along with every bale of hay, either," Luckett said. "Do you think he'd be interested in the job?"

"Oh, I'm sure he would!" Heather exclaimed. "It will be a fine opportunity for both of us."

"Good, good. Do you want me to talk to the mayor about it — when this problem with those outlaws has been cleared up, of course?"

"Please do — I'll appreciate it so very much! I don't expect to see Shawn until morning, and I'll tell him about it then. But in the meantime, anything you can do, all of you — I'll be so grateful. Shawn will, too, I know."

"We could get a committee together, call on Rufus," Mrs. Luckett suggested. "I'd ask some of the wives of the merchants —"

"Let me talk it over with him first," Luckett said, interrupting. "I'll take Pete Barkley along with me. And Ross Sargent. He was against giving in to the outlaws in the first place — him and Mason Ryder — and they're both on the town council. I'm sure we can count on them being all for it. If we can't swing Rufe over to our way of thinking, then we'll get a committee of townspeople together and call on him. He'll be in no position to refuse then."

And that's where the discussion had ended. Heather had gone to her room when the meal was over, filled with soaring thoughts of the future, of the life that she and Shawn could make for themselves in Yucca Flat.

Now, sitting on the edge of the bed in the quiet loneliness of her room, she told herself it was just as well there hadn't been time to tell Shawn of the good fortune that was about to befall them.

It would be better to think out ahead what she would say, how best to convince him that it was the thing to do. He still had it in mind to continue the search for his brother, and persuading him to abandon that could be difficult.

13

"Best goddamn rooms in this dump."

The voice sounded like that of the outlaw called Stinger Kenshaw, but Starbuck wasn't sure.

"Mayor said he was putting us up here, and it ain't costing us nothing!"

There was a noisy shuffling around the desk in the hotel's lobby. Shawn flattened himself against the wall, grateful for the darkness broken only slightly by the light from lamps entering the corridor from the forward area.

"Upstairs. Them'll be the best rooms."

Shawn watched one of the outlaws stagger into view, angle toward the stairs to the left of the clerk's desk. Another — Gabe Mather, it looked to be — was immediately behind him. Both men were very drunk. A third member of the gang shuffled into Starbuck's line of sight, but he was bent forward, face tipped down and unrecognizable.

They reached the steps, began a noisy ascent, and finally gained the upper floor. Standing in the deep shadows, Shawn could hear the solid thump of their boots as they moved along the hallway and searched for the rooms assigned them.

97

The thudding ended. A door slammed loudly. The men had located their quarters. At once Starbuck drew away from the wall and hurried toward the front of the building. He slowed his steps. He'd best go carefully; the rest of the Crissman bunch could be coming to the hotel, were possibly just outside on the gallery.

Shawn halted, the sound of steps followed by a splintering crash and a volley of oaths bringing him up short. The others were coming, one apparently having fallen over and demolished a chair on the porch.

Starbuck wheeled to retreat again into the darkness at the lower end of the hall. His eyes caught the corridor to his right, a short one. A door was vaguely visible at its termination. He turned into it at once, realizing it possibly was the alternate entrance to the building; the one he'd tried earlier was evidently a storage closet.

Reaching the panel, he turned the knob. The door swung back, and the cooling, fresh breath of the night greeted him. Grimly satisfied, Starbuck stepped out onto a small landing, noting that the hotel had a side rather than a rear exit — which was of no consequence; the important thing was that he was in the clear again, and gone unnoticed by Cobb Crissman and his followers.

Circling the building, Shawn returned to the sorrel, and swinging onto the saddle, rode the big gelding through the eerie quiet to Sargent's Livery Stable. Passing by the corrals, he entered the sprawling building, pungent with the odors of fresh hay, horses, and their droppings, and continued on for the front of the structure, where he could see a man sitting, chair cocked against a wall, beneath a lantern. At Shawn's approach along the runway, he came to his feet.

"Who is it?" Ross Sargent asked.

"Me — Starbuck."

The stable owner, smiling broadly, extended his hand as Shawn halted and dismounted before him.

"Want to shake your hand, Starbuck. . . . Any man that'd do what you've done's worth knowing."

"Not over yet."

"Maybe not, but you sure set Cobb Crissman and his bunch down hard on their tails! They ain't done nothing since Aaron Frisk and Norm Robinette rode in and told them what you said. Just laid around the Border Queen swilling rotgut. . . . Seen them heading for the hotel a bit ago. Turning in for the night, I reckon."

Starbuck shrugged. "Yeah, about run into them."

Sargent's eyes spread. "You been at the hotel?"

"Went there to see that fellow Leviticus. Had to make sure he'd be here in the morning to do his job."

The stableman whistled softly. "So that's what you're aiming to do — go ahead with the hanging! Sort of figured it was something like that when Aaron and Norm said you'd took Forsman away from them, but I was thinking you'd maybe figured to haul him off to some other town."

"Judge said it was to be done here, and you've got the gallows built. I'll be here in the morning at sunrise, with him."

"Where's he now — somewhere here in town?"

"Got him hid out in the hills."

"That's best, for sure. . . . This is really going to be something — and it's going to prove to Crissman and his kind that they can't tromp on the law anytime they take the notion."

"That's the whole idea. How about the others — Doc Schultz, Jorgenson, and that saloon man, Ryder? They still with us?"

"Can figure on Doc and Asa. Not too certain about Ryder. With that bunch making his place their hangout, he sort of hates to leave it."

"Told them to meet me at the hotel — picked it because they can't see the gallows from there — and there's a good chance they won't be bothering him. Anybody else we can depend on?"

"Not so far. How many men had we ought to have around?"

"Half a dozen at least if we're going to keep the odds right."

"Means I'll need to dig up two or three more. Expect I can do it. Know a couple that'll throw in with us once they see what's going on."

"Be needing a horse and wagon, too."

"What for?"

"Haul Forsman's body to the cemetery when it's over with. But I'll explain all that to you when the time comes. You talked with Teague since dark?"

"Sure have. He's madder'n a turpentined cat. Same goes for Barkley. They say your horning in like you have's going to mean real trouble for the town and that you hadn't ought to settle your grudge with Crissman at our expense. What's it all about, anyway? I sort of got the idea he was a stranger to you."

"He is," Starbuck said, shrugging. "I never saw him before in my life — only his kind. Guess you could call that the grudge. I don't like the Cobb Crissmans that're running loose in this country, and coming up against one always raises the hackles on my neck."

Sargent wagged his head slowly. "You sure got strong feelings about the law."

"Enough to know folks had better stand by it or else give up."

"That's what we're starting to learn — leastwise, some of us," the livery stable man said. "What do you want the rest of us to do in the morning?"

"There has to be witnesses to the execution — the hanging. That's the law. You and the men you can get to show up — armed — will be there at the gallows with Leviticus. I've warned him to keep quiet about this, and get there on time without being seen."

"Can go out the hotel by the back way, come down the alley . . ."

"That's what he'll be doing. Big thing is, we don't want Crissman or any of his bunch to know what's happening until it's all over."

"Going to be a little hard keeping it from them."

"Maybe not. They'll be at the hotel, and that's at the other end of the street. And, come sunrise, I expect to be standing out in front waiting for them when they come out."

Sargent's jaw sagged. "Alone?"

"No other way. If I'm backed up by half a dozen men with guns, there's sure to be some shooting, and I want to avoid that. By being by myself, that very fact will keep them quiet and staying put while Leviticus gets his job done.

"One of the reasons I stretched the truth a bit, made it sound to Crissman like I've got a bone to pick with him. He's probably been trying to remember me and what it is between us ever since he got my message."

Sargent laughed. "Sure done something to him! Like I said, he's been meek as a lamb far as hoorawing the town's concerned."

"Just hope I can keep him guessing until after it's all over in the morning. . . . Think you can scare up a bit of grub — enough for Forsman and me both? Biscuits and jerky'll be fine."

"Can do better than that — and right here in

102

my own kitchen. Stocked up my shelves a coupla days ago."

"Won't need much, and I can't build a fire to do any cooking. Afraid it might give away my hiding place. Not sure about Aaron and Norm. Got a hunch they'd like to double back and try taking Forsman off my hands. Aaron's out to get that marshal's job for himself, and Norm's all set to be his deputy. Bringing in Forsman — and me — would be a feather in their caps."

"That's a fact. Aaron's sure lagging for that job," Sargent said, taking Shawn by the arm and moving toward the rear of the stable, where he had living quarters. "Got coffee setting on the stove. Can take your fill while I get that grub together for you."

Starbuck, hanging onto the reins of the sorrel, continued the length of the runway with Sargent, paused when they reached a door to their left, one that apparently led into a second, smaller structure built off the main building.

Tethering the gelding in a nearby stall where he could munch on a manger of hay while waiting, Shawn watched while Ross lit a lamp, and then followed him into a fairly large room, one complete with bed, a couple of woven leather chairs, a table, and kitchen area. Sargent lived alone; such was evident not only from the meager furnishings but the stack of dirty pans and dishes on the sideboard near the stove and the stained clothing draped carelessly here and there over convenient protuberances.

"Grab yourself a clean cup, if you can find one," Ross said, motioning toward the stove, "and help yourself to the coffee."

Shawn filled a granite cup with lukewarm black liquid from the pot, settled in one of the chairs. Sargent, taking an empty flour sack, began to move about in front of the shelving built against the wall, dropping in whatever food that struck his fancy.

"Need only enough for tonight, maybe a bite or two in the morning," Starbuck said, noting the generous amounts the stableman was providing.

"No sense in going hungry — not that I give a tinker's damn whether Lem Forsman does or not."

"One thing," Shawn said, remembering, rising to his feet. Sargent, satisfied with his selection, moved toward him. "Can use a bottle of whiskey."

"Sure," Ross said, halting. Turning back, he took a near-full quart from one of the shelves, pressed the cork deeper into the neck of the glass container with a thumb, and added it to the items in the sack. "Nights get plenty sharp out there in the hills — mornings, too. Man needs a nip now and then to keep his blood circulating."

"The truth," Starbuck agreed, finishing off the coffee. He could have told Sargent the liquor was for Lem Forsman, not himself — a final treat, or perhaps an anesthetic, before he faced the noose — but he let it pass. Ross, like all others in Yucca Flat, would have little sympathy for the condemned man.

"Guess that fixes me up," he said, taking the sack from the stableman and moving for the door. "I'd like to —"

"You say something about paying me for that grub and I'll . . ."

Starbuck grinned. "All right, but I'm obliged to you just the same. . . . See you at sunup."

"I'll be waiting and ready, along with Doc and the others. Just come in the back way, like you did. I'll leave the doors open."

Shawn crossed to the stall where he'd left the sorrel. Backing the gelding into the runway, he went onto the saddle and swung the horse about. Nodding to Sargent, he rode the length of the barn to its exit, passed between the corrals and broke out into the open, and moments later was moving west for the road that led to the hills.

Reaching the last of the houses, Starbuck slowed, glanced over a shoulder, a feeling that he was being watched gnawing at his consciousness, and stirring into life within him an uneasiness. He could see no one, and absolute silence lay over Yucca Flat, with only the light in Ross Sargent's window breaking the darkness.

After a time he rode on through the gourd-scented night, but a man always attuned to his intuitions, he could not dismiss the belief that his departure from the settlement had been closely noted by someone. But there was nothing to be done about it other than keep an eye on his back trail during his return to Lem Forsman.

14

Starbuck rode wide of the old Taichert place, taking that precaution to throw off anyone who might be on his trail. A good distance beyond the shack, squatting gloomily in the shadows at the foot of the buttes, he veered from a due-south course, angled up the slope, and keeping high on the steep grade, doubled back to the twin pines where he had left Lem Forsman.

The outlaw began to strain and thresh wildly about when Shawn rode up and dismounted. Ignoring the man, Starbuck strode to the lower side of the boulder and its adjacent trees and listened into the night. He could hear no hoofbeats nor any other untoward sounds, and returning to the camp, he unhooked the flour sack of grub from the saddle and placed it on a rock close by. Moving then to Forsman, he removed the gag and unlocked one of the cuffs securing his wrists, allowing him to lower his arms and draw away from the tree. The outlaw unleashed a tirade of cursing the moment he was free.

"Shoulders are nigh to killing me!" he complained after the initial denouncement was over. "Ain't right to torture a man the way you're doing!"

Shawn made no comment, simply waited in

silence while Forsman moved his arms about to ease the cramped muscles, and then, restoring the steel cuff to the man's wrist, secured him again, this time with his hands in front. That completed, Starbuck dug into the flour sack.

"No fire, so it'll be a cold meal," he said, handing the bottle of whiskey to Forsman. "Maybe this will help."

The outlaw snatched the container from him, pulled the cork with his teeth, and tipping the bottle to his lips, took a long drink.

"It'll help, for damn sure," he said, smacking. "What've you got there to eat?"

Shawn laid out the food Ross Sargent had provided on the spread flour sack, and taking a chunk of bread and a slice of fried meat, sat down on a nearby rock. Forsman helped himself to the supply, wolfing his portions hurriedly, pausing in between mouthfuls to take a swig of the whiskey.

"You see Cobb and the boys when you was in town?" he asked when the edge was off his hunger.

Starbuck nodded.

"Bet you stayed plenty clear of them, didn't you?" the outlaw said with a grin, and then added: "Reckon they're just setting and waiting for me to show up."

"Expect they are."

"Well, one thing for damn sure, it ain't going to be me swinging at the end of that rope in the morning! You maybe are running this shebang

108

now, but comes tomorrow, it'll be a different story. More'n likely it'll be you hanging from that gallows."

"Wouldn't count on it," Shawn said calmly, and reaching for the bottle, had himself a drink of the whiskey.

"Who you figure's going to help you?" Forsman demanded. "Cobb's got that town buffaloed — scared stiff. There ain't nobody there that'll side you against him and the boys."

Starbuck drew up slowly, eyes narrowing. Somewhere on the slope below the pines a twig had snapped. Setting the bottle near the outlaw, he put the last of the meat he was eating into his mouth and casually got to his feet. No animal had created that sound — of that he was certain. It would have been a man. His thoughts flipped back to those moments earlier when he rode out of Yucca Flat and that feeling he was being watched; he hadn't been wrong.

"Smart thing for you to do is turn me loose now," Forsman went on. "You do that, and I'll put in a good word for you with Cobb. Ain't saying he'll listen to me, now, mind you — Cobb gets plenty all-fired riled up when he's crossed, but maybe this time he'll sort of forget it."

Shawn, ears straining, eyes covertly probing the shadowy brush surrounding them, turned away.

"You listening to me?" the outlaw shouted, his tongue thickening a little from the repeated dosages of liquor. "I'm trying to do you a favor!"

"Only favor you can do me is to shut up!" Starbuck snapped, and moved off toward the horses.

There had been no repeat of the noise he'd heard, but such was no guarantee of anything. A man endeavoring to sneak up on the camp, and making a careless mistake, was not likely to let it happen a second time. Senses keenly alert, Shawn halted by the horses. Both were contentedly munching the broad leaves of a jojoba bush as they took their ease in the cool half-dark.

Coming about quietly, Shawn stood unmoving in the night, glance continually searching the ragged area around the huge rock and the two pines. Forsman now lay half-upright, shoulders against the boulder, legs spread before him while he continued to nurse the bottle of liquor. Shawn wished he had remembered to pick up some rope while he was in town so that he could tie the outlaw's feet together. Such would have made Forsman less of a problem in the hours that were to come. As it was . . .

"Step out into the open, Starbuck!"

Shawn stiffened at the harsh command. The voice, a familiar one, came from the dense brush a few paces to his right. Jaw set, angered at being taken off guard despite the care he'd taken, Starbuck pulled away from the horses and walked slowly toward the trees and Lem Forsman. He still could not see who it was in the brush; certainly it was not one of Crissman's gang — which narrowed it down considerably. That left either Norm Robinette or Aaron Frisk as the logical prospects.

"Hold it right there," the voice ordered.

Shawn came to a halt in front of the outlaw, who had shaken off his lethargic state to some extent and was staring at him in a stupefied, wondering way.

"Now, real careful . . . drop your gunbelt."

It was Norm. Shawn recalled the voice, and as the man eased out of the brush and into view, recognition was no surprise. Unbuckling his cartridge-filled belt, Starbuck allowed it and his holstered weapon to fall.

"Step away from it," Robinette directed, waggling his pistol suggestively.

Cool in spite of the anger simmering within him, alert for any opportunity that would permit him to overcome the man, Starbuck fell back a stride or two. Forsman, finally aware that something was happening, had drawn himself to a sitting position and was focusing his wavering attention on Norm Robinette.

"Who the hell're you?" he mumbled.

"Just keep sitting where you are," Norm replied.

"You . . . you're one of them jaspers that come after me, ain't you?" the outlaw continued. "The one that's aiming to be a deputy?"

"That's me. Now, stay put, and soon as I take care of this bird, we'll light out for town."

"By God, I'm glad to hear that!" Forsman

yelled, and struggled to his feet. "I've took all the horsing around I'm going to!"

"Keep back — out of the way!"

"Not till I've rapped this here bottle over that bastard's head I ain't!" Forsman shot back, and lunged unsteadily toward Starbuck.

Shawn reacted instantly. He jerked to one side, put the outlaw between himself and Robinette. Norm fired the weapon in his hand hastily, but Starbuck was moving away, and the bullet went wide. Grabbing Forsman by the shoulders, Shawn shoved him at Robinette. Cursing, the would-be deputy dodged to keep from being knocked down.

Pivoting fast, Shawn threw a hurried glance to the ground, looking for his pistol. In the darkness he could not locate it, and there was no time for a search. Continuing the spin, he crowded in behind the floundering Forsman, reached for Norm, caught him by the wrist.

Robinette, endeavoring to jerk free, lashed out with his pistol at Starbuck's head. Shawn warded off the blow with his left arm, swung hard with the right at Norm's jaw. The darkness made it difficult to do much of anything other than grapple, and Forsman, stumbling about between them, made matters all the worse.

Fingers still locked about Robinette's wrist, Starbuck hung on. Abruptly Forsman lost his footing, fell clear. Shawn, feet firmly planted, leaned to the right, put all his strength into a hard jerk.

Robinette came up against his bent shape, tripped, went down. Immediately Shawn was on him, knees pressing into the man's back, pinning him to the ground. Starbuck, heaving for wind, saw the glint of the weapon in Norm's hand. He reached out as the man endeavored to bring it into play, caught it by the barrel, and wrenched it free.

Pulling back, Shawn came upright off Robinette, suddenly aware of the shadowy, weaving figure of Lem Forsman surging toward him. The outlaw had placed his hands together, was using the chain that linked the steel cuffs as a club.

Ducking Forsman's awkward swing, Starbuck looped a hard right at the outlaw's head. His fist landed solidly on the ear, and with a grunt, Lem dropped to the ground.

Starbuck swung his attention quickly to Robinette, now coming to his feet. He saw his own belted gun then, kicked to one side during the scuffling, and keeping the pistol he held trained on Norm, he bent, recovered it.

Robinette, sucking for breath, bits of leaves and twigs clinging to his features, glared at him from across the small clearing.

"Should've let me have him," he said wearily, brushing at his mouth with the back of a hand. "Hell, man, you can't get away with what you're doing. Crissman and his bunch'll never let you. Be you that'll get strung up, not him."

"And you'll be right there giving them a

hand," Shawn said in disgust. "You'll make a damn poor lawman, mister. The good ones fight for the law — not against it."

"Not doing it for him, but for the town."

"Town's duty is to see that he pays for what he's done. Wrong for it to crawl in a hole and hide just because half a dozen hard cases threaten it."

"You can say that — it ain't your town."

"But it's my law," Starbuck said quietly, "same as it's yours and every other man's in this country — and I don't aim to see it trampled on. Grab a hold of Forsman, drag him over to that pine tree."

Robinette hesitated briefly, and then, moving to where the outlaw lay, caught him under the armpits and moved him to the nearest of the two trees. As he was doing so, Shawn thrust the pistol he'd taken from Norm inside his waistband and quickly strapped his own weapon about his middle.

Norm, his chore finished, faced Starbuck. "You handcuffing me, too?"

Starbuck nodded coldly. "Would if I had another pair. Way I see it, you're no better than him."

"Only doing what I figured was needful. With the cards all stacked against us —"

"I've listened to all the excuses I intend to," Shawn snapped. "I've been in some towns where folks were up against a hell of a lot worse problem than Yucca Flat is, and still did the right thing. No reason why you people can't — if you'd put a little starch in your backbones. . . . I need some rope. Where'd you leave your horse?"

15

Robinette made a gesture toward the brush below the camp.

"Let's get him," Shawn said, and stepping in behind the man, trailed him to where he'd picketed his mount.

Untying the horse, Norm came slowly about, a quietness in his movements and manner. Starbuck smiled, shook his head.

"Don't try it. No reason for us to have it out, but if you push it, I'll shoot you down same as I will Forsman if he tries to make a break."

"You got no cause to hold me," Robinette declared belligerently. "I ain't one of them."

"Maybe not, but you put yourself in the same wagon when you jumped me."

"Only trying to do what Teague wanted. Turning Lem over to Crissman's for the good of the town."

Starbuck swore tiredly. "I'm not about to hash that over with you again! You know damn well it's not so. . . . Now, lead that horse back to camp, and if you make one wrong move, I'll put a bullet in you."

At once Norm started off, leading the buckskin he was riding by the short rope he'd looped to the bridle ring. When they reached the clear-

116

ing, Shawn gestured at the other horses.

"Over there."

Norm continued on, and under the eyes of Starbuck, tethered his mount alongside the sorrel and Forsman's bay.

"That lasso on your saddle — bring it," Shawn ordered.

Robinette, glumly silent, complied, and with Starbuck a step behind him, returned to where Forsman, empty whiskey bottle clutched by the neck, lay sprawled in drunken slumber.

"You won't be needing to tie me up," Robinette said, halting near the outlaw. "Can give you my word . . ."

Starbuck shook his head. It had been a long day, and it was beginning to tell on him.

"Sorry, but I can't take the chance. Too much riding on things going off without a hitch in the morning. Sit down there against the pine."

Norm's shoulders stirred in resignation, and crossing to one of the trees, he settled himself beside it. Taking the lariat, Shawn bound the man's hands and feet, threw a hitch around the pine's trunk, and with the trailing surplus, tied Lem Forsman's ankles together firmly. There was now no possibility of either prisoner making an escape, and with such assurance, he could get a little rest.

"You a lawman once?" Norm asked as Shawn drew back into the center of the clearing.

"Done a turn or two at wearing a badge. Never stayed with it for long."

117

"Sure act like one."

"Only doing what any man who believes in the law would do," Starbuck replied dryly, finding himself a comfortable place to sit.

Robinette stirred, shifted his position, already weary of the hard ground. "You sure are hell on that! A man'd figure Lem Forsman was the only killer there ever was!"

"He is, far as I'm concerned — and if you're aiming to wear a badge, you'd better start looking at it the same way."

"I . . . I don't know. Many as there is of his kind running loose, I don't see how it makes much difference. He'd get caught up with someday and get hisself hung anyway."

Starbuck rubbed impatiently at the stubble on his jaw. "That's what folks back where I come from call hunching a load. Means when there's a half-dozen men or so in a line moving a heavy timber, or maybe a rail, on their shoulders, one of them stoops a bit more than the others, making them bear his share of the weight."

"Ain't never yet backed off of doing my share!" Robinette said indignantly.

"That's what your town's doing — and you're part of it."

"Was what we were told to do, me and Aaron."

"And I'll give odds you knew it was wrong."

Norm stirred again. "Yeah, reckon I did, but when the mayor —"

"You have to learn to stand up against men

like him same as you do an outlaw when you know they're not doing right."

"Wouldn't keep a job for long, was I to try that!"

"Yes, you would. You'll find out most people usually want to see things done right, and they're willing to stand by you."

"They sure ain't showing it around here!"

"Only because you don't have an honest lawman taking charge. That deputy you had — Gallinger, I think his name was — appears to me was out to do the job the way it should be done, hiding Forsman when he got wind there was going to be trouble so's he'd be around for hanging.

"The law said Lem Forsman had to pay for the murder he did, and the oath Gallinger took when he pinned on his star bound him to seeing that the judge's sentence was carried out. That's the way it has to work, else the outlaws will run this country."

"You saying that if Dave was still around things wouldn't've got into the shape they are?"

"That's the way it looks to me. He, or that marshal Forsman killed, wouldn't bargain with Crissman, and they'd have gone ahead with the execution even if it meant a showdown with that bunch. The law has to be strong, otherwise it's not the law — it's just a bunch of rules written down on paper that nobody pays any attention to."

"Yeah, but Teague's the mayor, and it seems

to me if he figured —"

"Teague's a desperate man trying to do what he thinks is best, and hoping all the while he can dodge trouble."

"Rufe's done a lot for the town . . . worked hard . . ."

"Doesn't change the fact that dealing with Cobb Crissman to beat the law was wrong —"

"Well, then, what would you've done if you'd been him?" Norm broke in.

An owl hooted into the quiet night. Starbuck listened for a moment, shrugged. "I'll admit it's easy to talk, and no man ought to pass judgment on another at a time like this until he's stood in his boots, but I think I'd have got a bunch of the men together, as many as I could, and stood up to Crissman.

"Makes no difference if they are a bunch of gun-slingers, they'd back off if they were met by a dozen or so armed citizens ready to open up on them. Odds would be too high — and their kind always figure the odds. If they're not in their favor, they forget it. It's the cinch bets they go for."

Norm Robinette was silent for a long time. Then: "Got to say this, Starbuck, I'm kind of glad you come along and cut yourself in on this. It's set me to thinking."

Shawn nodded. His eyes were heavy, and despite the night's rising chill and the hard ground, he was close to sleep. The owl hooted again, the sound lonely, remote.

"Fire'd feel mighty good," Robinette said.

120

"Going to get plenty cold."

"Have to do without. Glare could attract somebody," Starbuck replied, rising stiffly.

"Who? Crissman and his bunch've holed up in the hotel. . . ."

"Far as we know," Shawn said, crossing to the horses and getting his blanket roll. "And there's Aaron Frisk."

"He won't be up and around — not Aaron. Can be sure he won't do nothing that'll stir things up any."

Starbuck shook out his blankets, laid one upon Robinette, the other over Lem Forsman, and resumed his place. Norm spat, pointed at the outlaw with his chin.

"No sense wasting that cover on him. Better keep it for yourself."

"The man's spending his last night on this earth. Guess he's entitled to a little comfort. . . . I won't need it, anyway. After soaking up heat in the Chihuahua Desert the way I've done, the cold feels sort of good."

Shawn lay back. Coyotes were yapping from the ledges of the higher country, and the owl voiced his mournful cry once more. Close by, a rustling in the dry leaves beneath the brush told of some small animal scavenging the bread scraps thrown there earlier by Forsman.

It would be good to see the first flare of daylight in the east. He could then head for town with Forsman and Norm Robinette, keep his grim appointment with Leviticus, the hangman, and be finished with the job he'd shouldered.

When it was over he'd start making inquiries about Ben, and if he'd not been seen, ride on, pointing for the next town that he might have gone to after crossing the border. Yucca Flat seemed the logical place, and he still had no good reason to think it was not.

Ben just might be in the settlement at that very moment, asleep in the hotel, perhaps, or the guest of some family, taking pity on him and the others with him after hearing of the ordeal they'd been through. For all he knew, Ben could have been somewhere along the street at the time he put Cobb Crissman in a cell and was later forced to release him. His brother could have been watching from a distance, and since no one except Heather Rustin knew that he was Shawn Starbuck during those moments, Ben would have been unaware of his identity.

But he'd change all that in the morning; in fact, he could start now. Pulling himself to one elbow, he peered through the weak starshine at Robinette.

"Norm . . ."

There was no response. Starbuck settled back. Robinette was asleep, and there was no need to awaken him. He'd let it ride until morning, do his checking when he reached town. Best he keep his mind on what lay ahead, anyway; facing up to Cobb Crissman and the rest of Lem's hardcase friends with no more backing than he'd mustered so far promised to be no easy task.

16

At the first sign of light, Starbuck was awake. Rising, he crossed to where the horses were picketed, and digging out of his saddlebags a sack of coffee beans, a cup, and the lard tin he used for boiling water, he hung a canteen on his shoulder and retraced his steps to the clearing.

He no longer need be wary of a fire, he felt; by the time anyone searching for him saw the smoke and could reach it, he would be well on the way to Yucca Flat with his prisoners.

Pulling a few stones together into an open-end circle, he built a fire of dry wood within them and set the can of water over the flames. His activity aroused Robinette, who sat up, began vigorously to chafe his hands despite the rope linking his wrists. Shawn, noting this, rose, and crossing to the man, freed his ankles. Making no move to also release Norm's hands, he nodded toward the flames.

"Get closer, soak up some of that heat. Coffee'll be ready in a couple of minutes."

Robinette struggled to his feet, and hurrying to the fire, squatted beside it, arms extended. Starbuck, halting beside Forsman, reached down, grasped the outlaw by the shoulder, and shook him awake.

Lem, eyes bloodshot, mouth slack, stared up at him. "What the hell you want?"

"Get up," Shawn ordered. "Coffee's about ready. You want something to eat?"

"Hell no, if it's some of them scraps you give me last night," Forsman said sourly. "Be getting me a regular meal when I get to town, anyway."

"Doubt that," Starbuck replied, and returned to the fire.

The water in the tin had risen to a boil, and setting it aside, he poured a liberal amount of crushed beans into it, restored it to its place over the flames. When the now dark and foamy liquid surged to the brim of the tin, he once again set the container aside so that its contents could settle and cool.

"What're you doing here?"

At Forsman's thick voice, Norm Robinette glanced up. Grinning dryly at the outlaw, he said, "Keeping you company."

Forsman stared blearily at the rope binding Robinette's wrists. "What's he taking you in for?"

"Reckon he don't trust me."

The outlaw shifted his attention to Starbuck, pouring a measure of coffee into the cup. "How about a little of that whiskey?"

"You finished it off last night. Better take some of this," Shawn said, offering the man the cup of steaming liquid.

"Hell with that!" Forsman snarled, and knocked the cup from Starbuck's extended hand. "When're we pulling out?"

"Soon enough," Shawn answered coldly, hanging tight to his temper. Picking up the container, he poured half of what was left in the lard tin into it, and passing it to Robinette, drank his share of the coffee from the tin.

Finished, he restored his equipment to its place in his saddlebags, rolled his blankets, and tightening the cinches of the saddles, brought up the horses. Lem Forsman, slouched against one of the pines, watched in surly silence.

"Mount up," Shawn directed, halting the bay in front of the outlaw.

"Ain't about to," Lem said with a broad sneer. "You want me on that nag, you put me on him."

"No problem," Starbuck snapped, and drawing his pistol swiftly, clubbed the outlaw smartly on the side of the head.

Surprised, stunned, Forsman cursed, slumped against the tree, but as Shawn moved toward him a second time, he hurriedly grabbed the horn of his saddle and heaved himself onto the bay.

Shawn, taking a loop around the outlaw's middle with the rope, cinched it tight with an extra dally, and turned to Robinette. Norm was already on his horse, a half-grin on his bearded face.

"You ain't getting no argument from me," he said.

In no mood for humor, Starbuck only nodded, and drawing the knife from inside his boot, he sliced off the tag end of the lariat and attached it to the bridle of Forsman's bay. Swinging onto his sorrel, he attached the rope to his saddle horn and moved out in front of the outlaw, forming a connected line in which he led, while Lem occupied the center, and Robinette, who he figured probably didn't need to be in the pack-train arrangement at all, brought up the rear. But as always, he would take no chances at such moments.

"I'm going to take all this damned foolishness out of your hide when we get to town," Forsman warned as they moved off down the slope. "I'm making Cobb turn you over to me, let me work you over real special."

"Best thing you can do, Lem, is start praying," Robinette said. "This here's one time you ain't getting away with what you've done."

"Me — swing? Not much, I ain't! Gallows ain't been built that I'll ever hang from."

Shawn, leading the way down the grade, began to veer more to the north. It would be better to avoid entering Yucca Flat by the main road in the event Crissman or some of his toadies took it upon themselves not to wait at the hotel but come out in an advance party and ambush him. He doubted the probability of such, but again he would take nothing for granted.

The slope slid off into an arroyo thickly bordered with Apache plume, rabbitbush, and globes of yellow-flowered snakeweed. He fol-

126

lowed its course until it began to swing west toward a second row of hills. There he changed direction, and pulling up out of the sandy wash, headed east.

He was above the road now, in ragged brakes country, and could come into the settlement from its northern end. Such would place Ross Sargent's livery stable first in line as he approached the town's twin rows of buildings, giving him a distinct advantage. Shawn glanced to the low, sprawling hills far to his right. The pearl glare above them was brightening, and color was beginning to show. They'd make town only a few minutes before sunrise.

It wouldn't hurt to be there a bit ahead of the time he'd planned, Starbuck decided, thinking of what yet had to be done, and raking the sorrel with his spurs, he broke the big gelding into a slow lope. Forsman's bay hung back at first, fighting the pull on his bridle, but shortly he fell into a matching pace, which was joined by Robinette's buckskin, and in a compact string they began to narrow the distance separating them from the blur of buildings and trees now taking form in the gray light.

The flat they were crossing began to slope, soon dropped down into another arroyo, one choked by a thicket of wait-a-minute acacia, and swinging around it, Starbuck angled directly for the settlement, approaching the scatter of structures steadily, with the weathered bulk of Sargent's stable rising between them and effectively closing off the view of anyone along the street who might be watching.

Reaching the corrals, Shawn led the way down the narrow lane that separated them, and rode into the rear of the stable. Darkness still claimed the interior of the structure. The front doors had been closed, and only a lantern hanging from a peg at mid-point along the runway spread any light. Shawn, guiding the sorrel toward it, pulled to a halt when he came abreast.

"Ross!" he called, a thread of doubt stirring through him. Sargent should be there waiting, along with the party of men he had recruited to assist in the execution.

"Who you hollering for?" Forsman asked sneeringly. "Ain't nobody in this town going to lift a hand to help you — not with Cobb and the boys setting out there just hoping somebody'll start something. Told you all along you was treeing the wrong cat."

Starbuck came off the sorrel, headed him into the nearest stall. Light was now seeping through the crack edging the barn's double doors. He realized sunrise was at hand.

"Climb down," he ordered, jerking on the rope attached to the outlaw.

Forsman dismounted with a swaggering flourish, broad teeth showing between his lips in a triumphant grin.

"Told you! Told you the only hanging that'd be done around here would be your'n!"

Starbuck glanced at Robinette. The man was

128

off his buckskin, was awaiting instructions. Jaw set, Shawn turned for the doors. If he'd lost, if Ross Sargent and the others had failed him, he'd know it immediately when he pushed open the heavy wooden panels and stepped outside, for Cobb Crissman and the rest of the outlaws would be waiting.

Left hand riding the butt of the pistol strapped to his leg, the other holding onto the rope connected to Forsman and Norm Robinette, Starbuck halted at the doors. A coolness had come over him now, replacing the feeling of chagrin and frustration that had filled him moments earlier. If he and John Leviticus were to do the job alone, then that was how it would be. He'd go as far as he could before he'd let them stop him.

Removing his hand from his gun, Starbuck grasped the crossbar securing the doors. Sliding it free of its brackets, he allowed the left panel to swing back. As it drifted slowly away, admitting a flood of light, he dropped his hand again to his weapon and stepped into the open.

A long sigh slipped from his lips. The street lay silent and deserted before him. Ross Sargent, Leviticus, and two other men were standing beside the gallows.

17

Lem Forsman began to curse wildly, struggle with the manacles that linked his wrists, and strain at the rope encircling his waist. Starbuck pushed him toward Ross Sargent and the other men hurrying toward him.

"Two?" he heard John Leviticus say. "Was told there'd be one."

"Only one," Shawn said.

"Was beginning to worry," Sargent said, throwing a nervous glance down the street. "Was expecting you earlier, and when you didn't show up, we got to wondering . . ."

Starbuck began to remove the rope from around Forsman's waist. The outlaw was now standing mute, staring at the grim, square out-line of the gallows with its overhead beam from which a readied noose was stirring stiffly in the early-morning breeze.

"Took a roundabout way getting here in case Forsman's friends took it into their heads to be waiting. Cost me a little time."

Ross nodded, glanced to the eastern horizon. The sun was just breaking over the rim of hills. "Reckon the time ain't really that important now. You got him here," he said, and shifted his attention to Robinette. "What've you got him tied up for?"

"Showed up last night. Had a notion to take Forsman away from me, turn him over to Crissman — like the mayor wants."

"Changed my mind about that," Norm said. "I'm admitting I was wrong — plenty wrong."

"Expect he means it," Shawn said, tossing the loose end of the rope to Robinette. "Just couldn't afford to take any chances."

Beyond the stableman, Leviticus, with the aid of Doc Schultz and Asa Jorgenson, was hustling the outlaw toward the scaffolding. Forsman was again struggling, fighting every step, while a stream of invectives poured from his lips.

"What about it, Norm?" Shawn heard Sargent ask. "You with us . . . or against us?"

"Count me on your side," Robinette replied. "Sort of got a good look at myself last night, listening to Starbuck. Made me realize what me and some of the others around here was doing — or aiming to do."

Sargent rubbed at his jaw. "This for sure? This here thing's sort of touch and go, and we can't risk no trouble with you."

"You've got my word, Ross."

"All right," Sargent said, letting his hand fall away from the pistol he had strapped on. "You can get that rope off."

Starbuck, his face a deep study, turned to the stable owner. "This all you could get to help — Doc Schultz and Jorgenson?"

"Best I could do," Ross said heavily. "Talked

131

to half a dozen others — men I figured I could trust to keep their mouths shut. Got turned down by them all."

Starbuck shrugged wearily.

"Reckon we can't blame them too much," Sargent continued apologetically. "First time they've ever been up against a bunch like Crissman's, and they're feared something'll go wrong."

"Nothing like that's going to happen," Starbuck said, facing Robinette, now free of the rope. Drawing the pistol he'd taken from him the night before, he returned it. "You'll maybe be needing this. Ross'll tell you what to do."

Pivoting, he looked again to the gallows. Asa Jorgenson, by sheer strength, was forcing the struggling Lem Forsman up the steps. Leviticus, already on the landing, one hand steadying the noose, waited patiently. Schultz had taken his place at the edge of the platform, beneath the floor, a position evidently assigned him by the hangman. Somewhere in the town a rooster crowed.

Starbuck glanced toward the sun. It was above the horizon, showing brilliant white and blotting out the surrounding sky above and land below with its blinding glare.

"Everybody know what's to be done?" Shawn asked, coming back to Sargent.

"Was just explaining it to Norm," Ross said. "Soon as the hanging's over, we put Forsman in the coffin and load it on the wagon. Then Doc heads down the street for the graveyard, and we scatter out behind him. You'll be in front of the hotel."

"That covers it. Keep your gun in your hand."

Forsman, by dint of Jorgenson's efforts, was now on the landing and standing before the noose. He had ceased fighting the big man, seemingly had finally resigned himself to what lay ahead. And then abruptly he jerked away.

"Cobb!" he yelled in a high, cracked voice. "Cobb Crissman! I'm down here!"

One of Jorgenson's broad hands clapped over the outlaw's mouth with solid force, silencing him instantly. The other grasped a shoulder, propelled Forsman back to where he faced the noose. Shawn flung a quick glance at Norm Robinette.

"Take a look down the street, see if anybody heard him."

Robinette wheeled, trotted forward into the center of the lane separating the buildings, to a point where he could see beyond the bend.

"Nobody in sight," he called back.

Starbuck switched his gaze to the gallows. Forsman was motionless, staring wooden-faced at the wall of the structure directly before him. Leviticus dropped the rope about his neck, adjusted it carefully. Reaching then into an inside pocket of his coat, he produced a black satin hood, and leaning forward slightly, offered it to the outlaw. Forsman ignored the man stonily.

The hangman turned, glanced at the men on the ground below, nodded, and laying his hand on the trap lever, gave it a firm jerk.

Shawn looked away, pushing back the revulsion that welled through him, quieting it with the thought that such was necessary — that it was the only course open to men if the law was to prevail.

"Up to me now," he said, drawing his pistol and checking the cylinder to be certain it was fully loaded and that its action was free.

Sober, Ross said, "Don't like you going down there and facing that bunch alone. Feel like the rest of us ought to be backing you."

"If we do it that way, there's sure to be a shootout," Starbuck replied, watching Jorgenson bring up the wagon. "Best you let me handle it the way I've figured."

"Whatever you say," the livery stable man murmured.

The rooster crowed again, now to the accompaniment of several others. Shawn listened briefly, said, "How long will it take you?"

"Time we get the coffin nailed shut and Doc reaches the hotel . . . no more'n fifteen minutes, I'd say. That all right?"

"Be fine. . . . Good luck."

Shawn heard the like responses of the other men as he wheeled, moved off into the street.

Gaining the end of the near sidewalk, Starbuck proceeded slowly, making no grandiose show of striding boldly down the center of

134

the dusty roadway. He could see movement inside some of the stores through the windows, but there was no one visible in the open — and no one on the porch of the hotel, he saw, moments later, when the structure came into view.

The outlaws had taken upstairs rooms, he recalled. They could be watching him from that vantage point and in a position to cut him down easily if they were so inclined. But that possibility did not trouble him greatly; Crissman and the men with him, curious as well as confident of their hold on the town, would play out the hand the way he'd outlined and put in an appearance on the hotel's gallery.

He pressed on deliberately, casually, in the full blast of the sun. A coolness had settled over him after he'd covered those first dozen strides, and his mind was now devoid of all other thought, and dead center on what he was about to face.

He could be wrong about Cobb Crissman, and his outlaw followers were completely unpredictable, given cause. His plan could backfire, leave him standing literally naked before them and their guns. Nor could he expect too much from Sargent and the men with him — a doctor, a feed-store merchant, and a man who, perhaps, still wavered as to where his loyalties lay.

A phrase that he'd heard, or perhaps read, at some time during the past trickled through his mind. *No man stands alone when armed with the majesty of the law.* The remembrance brought a hard smile to Shawn's lips. Those were lofty, high-flown words; but did they have meaning where men like Cobb Crissman were concerned?

And then it came to him: that was what this was all about. Unknowingly, in his determination to see that a convicted criminal received the punishment due him according to the law, he was strengthening that law, giving it significance and proving it to be a shield of protection for those who believed in it and a force to be feared by those who did not — and that *was* the majesty of the law.

The hotel was just ahead, standing bleak and deserted-looking in the harsh sunlight. Off among the houses to the west of the settlement a cow lowed anxiously for attention. Such probably reflected the story of everyone in Yucca Flat at that moment; all else was forgotten as they looked on, wondering, and waiting to see what would happen.

Was Ben among them? Could he be somewhere along the street in one of the stores, or standing in a passageway, or possibly looking on from a room in the hotel? If so, would he recognize him as his brother? Few, other than Heather Rustin and the men who were standing by him, knew his name; to practically everyone in Yucca Flat he was a stranger, and any question put to them concerning his identity would go unanswered. Would he also be a stranger to his own brother?

Starbuck came to a halt. He had reached the

front of the hotel. Again, as always at such moments, his mind cleansed itself of all thoughts except those pertinent to the immediate situation. Settling himself squarely in the dust of the street, he faced the empty porch, the door beyond which lay the dark lobby.

"Crissman!" he called. "I'm here!"

18

Starbuck's words echoed hollowly along the street. Arms folded across his chest, he waited, eyes probing the windows, the corners of the porch, as well as the entrance to the structure.

"Crissman!"

Abruptly the hotel's sagging screen door flung back, banging hard against its frame. Cobb Crissman, hat cocked forward on his head, hands hanging at his sides, sauntered out onto the gallery. Close behind him came the remaining members of the gang: Denver Jessel, Baker, Job Roanoke, Kenshaw, and Gabe Mather. Shawn noted each, wanting to be certain all were present, that the outlaw chief had not stationed one or two at strategic points from which they could cover him with their guns.

They had been standing just inside the hotel's entrance, he guessed, looking him over and having their wonder as to his purpose.

"All right, I'm here," Crissman said, as his men fanned out around him. "What do you want?"

"You, mostly," Starbuck replied coolly.

Crissman swore, spat into the dust. "What the hell's this all about?" he demanded impatiently. "I know you from somewheres? We maybe have us a ruckus back in Dodge? Seems I sort of recollect you from there."

"No. . . ."

"Then, goddamnit, mister, speak up! If you've got a bone to pick with me, let's hear about it!"

"Just what it is — and it's between you and me. . . ."

The hotel's door swung open again, and Rufus Teague bustled out onto the porch. His features were taut, showed agitation, and his disarrayed clothing indicated a hurried dressing.

"Want you to remember!" he shouted, pointing a finger at Crissman. "I ain't got nothing to do with this! It's all that fellow's doings. I was willing to hand Forsman over to you, but he went and horned in and took him away from my deputies. You can't hold me and the town responsible for any of this!"

"Keep your shirt on, grandpa," Crissman drawled. "I ain't —"

"I'm holding you to your word! You promised me you wouldn't do no damage to the town or hurt nobody, and I'm expecting you to stand by it."

"That was yesterday," the outlaw said. "Now, get out of the way and go on about your business."

"This here town *is* my business."

Gabe Mather took a step forward. Grasping Teague by the arm, he swung the older man about, sent him reeling toward the door.

"Get back inside!" Mather snarled. "You

come butting in again and I'll nail your hide to the wall of this here fleabag."

Teague, recovering his balance, drew back the screen and disappeared into the interior of the hotel. Several of the outlaws laughed, and Crissman, pushing his hat to the back of his head, moved forward to the edge of the porch and leaned indolently against one of the roof posts.

"Ain't heard no answer from you yet," he said. "What's sticking in your craw . . . and where's Lem?"

"He'll be here," Starbuck replied. The faint thump of hammering back near Sargent's stable had ended. The wagon would be coming shortly. "Best we get something straight. Any one of your bunch gets an itchy trigger finger and puts a bullet in me, it's all off. Means you'll never know what I've got to say. Want that clear."

Crissman shook his head slowly. "You're stalling, friend. Like to know what for," he said suspiciously.

"Just want to get everything squared away."

"Well, you best start. I'm getting plenty tired of standing here listening to your yammering. Reckon you know I don't have to wait if I don't want to. Be no sweat going after Lem myself. Fact is, me and the boys'd sort of be pleasured doing just that, but you got me wondering why you're pulling this."

"Whyn't we forget about this jasper and start looking for old Lem?" Stinger Kenshaw suggested. "Sort of work us up a appetite was we to —"

"You gave me your word!" Rufus Teague shouted from beyond the hotel's door. "Man hadn't ought to go back on his promise!"

Shawn, nerves taut, listened for the rumbling sound that would tell him the wagon bearing Lem Forsman's body was on the way and that Ross Sargent, Asa Jorgenson, and hopefully, Norm Robinette were moving into position along the street. Such must be soon; he could hold Cobb Crissman's attention but little longer.

Movement in a window of the hotel's upper floor caught his eye. He raised his glance. Heather, with one of the women he'd seen on the porch when they first rode into town, was looking down at him. The girl lifted her hand, waved. He nodded slightly, lowered his attention, and settled it once more on the outlaws.

"You in El Paso six months or so ago?" he asked, pulling a question out of thin air.

Crissman shifted his stance, frowned. "El Paso? Could be. I ain't much good at remembering. Why? That where we met up?"

"Not the only place. I've seen the likes of you in plenty of towns."

The low rumble of the oncoming wagon was definite now, but it was still beyond the bend in the street and not yet visible.

"What's that mean?"

"Hell, he ain't got Lem!" Mather declared in a

141

loud voice. "He's just horsing us around — that's all. Let's get started —"

"Expect he's got him, all right," Crissman said, waving the outlaw back. "What I'm trying to find out is why — and I'm getting goddamn tired of asking over and over."

"Just waltzing us around the mulberry bush. . . ."

"Leading up to something, I reckon."

"That it?" Crissman asked. "That what this's all about?"

Starbuck nodded.

"Well, I'm done waiting, whatever you're doing. If Lem ain't standing here in front of me inside of two minutes, we're going to start taking this town apart board by board till we find him!"

"No!" Rufus Teague's anguished voice came from inside the hotel. "You gave me your word!"

Gabe Mather wheeled to face the cry. "You best keep your trap shut, old man! Could be we'll start with this here shack you call a hotel!"

"What the hell's the use of waiting two minutes?" Baker shouted, drawing his pistol. "It ain't going to make no difference. He ain't got Lem . . . was only bluffing."

Crissman wagged his head. "Can see that," he said, "but I'm still wondering what all the foofaraw's about — what he's got up his sleeve."

Starbuck, raising his arm slowly, brushed away the beads of sweat on his forehead. The wagon was rounding the turn in the street. Doc Schultz was on the seat, reins clutched tight in his hands. Beyond him, movement in the mouth of the passageway between the Border Queen Saloon and Purdy's Bakery indicated that one of the men had stationed himself at that point.

There would be someone inside the Eagle Café, directly opposite the hotel — Ross Sargent, he thought, had chosen that spot. A third man, if there was one, would have circled wide and taken a place within the vacant building adjoining it.

That was how it was supposed to be — the way he'd planned it with them; but there was no absolute guarantee it had worked out. With only the four of them, assuming Norm had not backed down — it was best they not count on Doc Schultz, whose job it was to drive the wagon — he could not blame any one of them for withdrawing at the last minute.

Facing up to six hardened killers like the Crissman gang, flaunting them, in reality, for the sole purpose of proving to them that the law meant something, was asking much, Shawn knew. But it was necessary, and for his part the point of no return had now been reached; Schultz and the wagon, with the raw-pine-board box containing the body of the outlaw in its bed, was now only a few strides away.

"What's that?" the thick-shouldered Kenshaw asked as the approaching vehicle caught his attention.

"Funeral," Baker replied. "They're carting some jasper off to the boneyard."

Cobb Crissman, eyes narrowing, pulled himself fully erect. Anger and suspicion tightening his features, he stared at Shawn.

"Who's in that coffin?"

"Lem Forsman — man you came for," Starbuck said calmly. "The law's through with him. He's all yours now."

19

Crissman was a taut, outraged figure poised on the edge of the hotel porch. Behind him his friends gaped in openmouthed consternation, seemingly unable to believe that anyone would dare oppose them.

"Reckon I savvy now what's been going on," said Cobb Crissman, anger tightening his voice. "All this stalling was so's your friends could lynch —"

"Was no lynching," Starbuck cut in coldly. "Lem was sentenced by a judge for murder. A hangman was sent to do the job. We only saw to it that he got to perform the execution."

"Was a lynching, all the same!" the outlaw named Baker declared, stepping up beside Crissman. "And we ain't letting nobody get away with stringing up a friend of ours! . . . Let's clean out this burg, boys!"

"Wait!" Starbuck warned. "Before you make up your minds to help a dead man, better take a look around. There's guns pointed at you — and they're ready to open up if you start anything."

The outlaws, crowding forward and coming off the porch slowed, halted, let their glances travel along the street. From the doorway of the Eagle Café came the glint of light on a rifle barrel. A man sprawled on the slanting roof of the vacant building directly opposite them stirred, made his presence known by exposing himself slightly above its edge. And at the corner of the bakery Ross Sargent, also with a rifle, stepped clearly into view. Shawn heaved a silent sigh. The man on the roof was Robinette; Norm had not backed out.

"No need for you hanging around here any longer," Starbuck continued. "I don't figure Lem Forsman is important enough to you, dead, to get killed over — if even he was when alive. Point is, he got what was coming to him according to the law, and nothing you can do now will change that."

Baker, his boyish features more mature in the harsh sunlight, sneered. "What are you, mister, some kind of a preacher?"

"I'm just another man wanting to see the law upheld and that right's done," Starbuck replied coolly. "There's plenty more like me around, and the sooner you learn that, the better off you'll be."

Raising a hand, he motioned to Schultz, who had pulled the wagon to a halt, to move on, taking care, not for an instant, to remove his eyes from the outlaws.

"Only thing left for you to do is get on your horses and ride out. Nothing for you here but trouble — and maybe a hangman's rope if it turns out you had something to do with the disappearance of the deputy."

"They done it — ain't no doubt!" a man shouted, coming suddenly from the passageway alongside Kinney's Hardware Store. "I'm the new marshal here, and I ain't letting them just go free!"

Starbuck stiffened in alarm. It was Aaron Frisk, and the shotgun he gripped in his hands was at full cock, the tall, rabbit-ear hammers standing up high like slightly curved towers. It would take very little to set off the outlaws, and a rash appearance such as Frisk was making could be the spark that accomplished it.

"There's no proof of that," Shawn warned. "We don't know that he's dead; and until we do, you'd best not accuse anybody. . . . Now, back off!"

Frisk, near the center of the street, halted. Schultz was continuing on his way to the cemetery at the edge of town, and now people were beginning to appear along the sidewalks, gathering in small groups.

"Mount up and pull out now," Starbuck said, attention again on Crissman. "We don't want trouble. The law's satisfied, and there's no sense pushing things any farther."

"Well, maybe we ain't satisfied," Baker said. "Lem was my friend, and I ain't about to forget you strung him up."

Cobb Crissman raised a hand, motioned the young outlaw to silence. He half-turned, let his glance touch Jessel, Kenshaw, and the others standing beside him. All seemed to be waiting for word from him as to what they should do next. Only Cass Baker was ignoring the outlaw leader. If there was to be trouble, it would start with the younger man, Shawn realized.

"He's right," Crissman drawled indifferently, as if they had been discussing a matter of little import. "Ain't no reason for us to hang around here, and Lem sure wasn't such a good pal that I'm willing to pull iron over — 'specially since he's croaked. . . . Let's move out."

"What about paying for all the damage you done around here?" Rufus Teague, taking courage from the trend of the situation, shouted as he burst out onto the hotel's porch. "And them rooms you used — I get two dollars a night —"

The outlaws came to a halt, and all the signs of sudden violence again hung in the air.

"Forget it, mayor!" Starbuck snapped. "The town can take care of it all."

Crissman's shoulders relented, and after a moment he moved on. The men, fanned out behind him in a close half-circle, quickly tense and poised like coiled springs awaiting only to be released at the interruption, resumed their slow progress — all but Cass Baker.

"I ain't for this, Cobb," he said in a low voice. "Us calling it quits and just walking off after what they done."

"Forget it, kid," Crissman said. "We ain't holding the right cards."

"I ain't for letting them go either!" Aaron Frisk declared, breaking into the tense moments again. "What's eating you, Starbuck? You been jawing and yapping about the law and how it's got to be upheld — and here you are turning that whole bunch loose!"

"Nothing to hold them for," Shawn said, striving to pacify the man. Sweat was lying thick on his forehead, but raising his hand to brush it away could be a mistake. "All they've done is break a few windows, make a nuisance of themselves. . . . We can overlook that."

"I say we can't — not if we're going to keep this town clean. I say we got them dead to rights and just where we want them, and we ought to crack down on them right where they're standing so's others of their kind'll know they can't come in here and do what they damn please!"

Cobb Crissman and the men with him had slowed their steps once more. Baker, now a short distance behind them, had wheeled slowly, was facing Frisk.

"You got a powerful big mouth, marshal," he said in a grating voice. "Maybe you'd like to come get me, throw me in your calaboose."

"He ain't the marshal!" Rufus Teague called anxiously, his attitude changing again. "Only talking for himself. . . . You boys just keep right on going. We're forgetting everything."

The tension hanging over the street was almost tangible. Starbuck, fighting for every passing moment, hopeful that no one would make the wrong move that would ignite the powder keg of violence upon which they all stood, turned once again to Frisk.

"Let it drop, damn you!"

"You ain't running this town! You're —"

"You ain't either, Aaron!" Teague shouted from the hotel's porch. "You're wanting to pin on Arlie Pringle's badge, but you ain't showing enough sense to wear it!"

"By letting them murderers go? That going to prove I can be a lawman? You better start thinking straight yourself, Rufe, not be listening to this here drifter who maybe ain't no better'n them killers when you come right down to it."

"You're talking crazy, Aaron."

"I'm only one making sense," Frisk declared. "We've got that bunch right where we want them — in a pocket with plenty of guns looking at them. Now's the time to cut them down, fix it so's they won't never bother us or anybody else again!"

"Telling you for the last time, Frisk — back off," Starbuck said, his voice carrying through the hot stillness.

From the lower end of the street where lay the cemetery, the solid thump of a pick could be heard. Doc Schultz had gotten the town sexton to work, and the grave for Lem Forsman was being prepared.

Everyone seemed to pause, listen to the hollow, measured sound as it echoed faintly along the buildings. The dull thud appeared to serve as a grim reminder and perhaps a spur to Cobb Crissman. Abruptly he resumed his agonizingly slow walk toward the horses tethered to the rack beyond the Border Queen. The men with him tarried briefly, followed suit, Baker, thumbs hooked in his belt, shoulders swaggering, included.

"You ain't going nowhere!" Aaron Frisk yelled suddenly, and swung the shotgun to his shoulder.

In the next fragment of time he was staggering backward and falling against the wall of Kinney's, as Baker, pivoting, drawing, and firing in a blur of motion, drove two bullets into his body before he could trigger the double barrel.

Instantly the street erupted in a hammering of guns.

20

Starbuck lunged, threw himself into the dust, and drew as he saw Cobb Crissman wheel to face him. The outlaw had his weapon out. Shawn saw it buck in his hand, felt a rush of wind as the bullet skimmed his face. He triggered a hasty shot, missed also. Instinctively he rolled to the side, destroying any possibility of being an easy target for Crissman, and fired again. But Cobb was dodging by him, legging it for the hotel.

Starbuck bounded to his feet. He could hear the screaming of women through the blasting of guns and smoke, and the smell of burned powder was beginning to hang in the air. As he spun to follow Crissman, he noted the outlaw Jessel sprawled face-down on the ground. A short distance beyond him, Gabe Mather was on one knee, holding his pistol with both hands as he fired methodically at Norm Robinette on the roof of the empty building.

Shawn reached the hotel porch, crossed to the door, drew up close to the wall at its side. Cobb could be waiting just inside, gun ready. Grasping the latch handle of the screened panel, he jerked it open. There was no answering blast of a weapon, and, hunched low, Starbuck plunged through into the dark lobby and dropped behind one of the large chairs.

Breathless, he waited for some reaction from the outlaw. None came, and then a hoarse voice called from behind the heavy portieres that separated the restaurant from the hotel proper.

"Upstairs — he went upstairs!"

Starbuck swung his attention to the speaker. It was Rufus Teague. His right hand was clasped to the upper part of his left arm, and blood was oozing out from between his fingers. Somehow he'd gotten in the way of a bullet.

Upstairs. . . . Shawn, taking a moment to reload his weapon, threw a glance to the top of the steps. The area was dark, offered only death. Cobb Crissman likely was waiting somewhere along the hallway that would be extending the length of the building; or he could be hiding in one of the rooms behind a partly open door. . . . But speculation accomplished nothing. The fuse had been lit by Aaron Frisk, and guns were now the only solution.

Keeping low, Starbuck edged his way around the chair, darted suddenly to a second one placed near the foot of the steps. Teague had pulled back into the restaurant area, where he was probably being cared for, and except for the sporadic crackle of rifles and pistols coming from the street, there was silence in the hotel.

Pressed tight against the stairway's picketlike banister, Shawn probed the shadows above with straining eyes. He could see nothing, only a rising wall of near-total blackness. Grim, jaw set, he started around the newel, hesitated as the cushion in the nearby chair caught his attention. Reaching out, he grasped it firmly in his right hand, and weapon ready in the left, he began the stair's ascent.

Midway, he halted. He was at the point where his head was level with the upper floor. Hunched close to the wall, he searched again for some indication of the outlaw's whereabouts, failed. The darkness was too deep. He could determine only the dim outline of the opening where the corridor began. But Cobb Crissman would be there, somewhere, waiting.

Bending down, he thumped the toe of his boot against the face of a step, and threw the seat cushion into the hallway. Instantly there followed a blinding orange flash and the thunderous clap of a pistol, the sound magnified a hundred times by its close confinement.

It had come from the far end of the narrow passageway lying between the rooms. Moving fast before the layers of hanging smoke could drift, Starbuck raced up the last of the steps and dropped flat on his belly at the beginning of the hall.

The aisle of darkness was before him. Hugging the worn carpeting, he endeavored to locate the outlaw; again failed. Crissman could be standing hard against a wall; he possibly was hunched low in a back corner, or he could, as Shawn had suspected earlier, be waiting inside a room.

The unquestionable possibility of a trap and

the foolhardiness of daring such was apparent. Shawn twisted half-way about, seeking an alternative. On the wall behind him, in the off-set between the two rooms fronting on the street, he could see the rectangular outlines of a window. Its heavy green fabric shade had been pulled down full length, covering it completely and effectively blocking out the light.

Still belly-flat, Starbuck wormed his way back into the offset. Drawing close to the wall, and still prone, he reached for the circular finger grip at the end of the cord dangling from the thick covering. Pulling it to its fullest extent, he released it. The shade flew up with a noisy scrape, fluttering wildly as the spring inside the wooden tube unwound itself.

Light flooded into the hallway. Starbuck, waiting, eyes riveted to its far end, saw Crissman spring erect, grab the knob of a door that opened out apparently onto the landing of the back stairs. The weapon in the outlaw's hand roared again, shattering the window behind Shawn, who fired fast at Crissman's moving shape as it vanished into the opening. Cursing as the door slammed shut on the heels of Cobb Crissman, Starbuck leaped upright, uncertain whether his bullet had scored or not.

He hesitated briefly, realizing it would be equally as foolish to follow the outlaw onto the landing as it would have been to trail him into the dark depths of the corridor. Pivoting, he gained the head of the stairs, plunged to their bottom. Turning into the lobby, he ran into the hall leading off it, reached the side entrance he'd used that previous night. Crouched low, he opened the door and stepped into the open.

He glanced to the rear of the building. There was no one in sight, nor could he see anyone in the opposite direction, beyond the porch. The shooting along the street had dwindled to only an occasional report, and he guessed that Ross Sargent and the others were hunting down the scattered outlaws who had undoubtedly taken cover among the buildings.

Still bent low, and hurrying, Starbuck moved along the side of the structure, halted when he came to its rear corner. Peering around the weathered boarding, he looked to the top of the flight of stairs that led up from the alley to the second floor. Crissman was not on the landing or on the steps. The outlaw, evidently unhurt, had descended, was now somewhere along the alley or possibly had ducked into the adjoining building.

Swiping at the sweat misting his eyes, impatient at the way it had all turned out, Shawn hunched low again, rounded the end of the hotel, and crossed to a large box — one partly filled with firewood — standing behind the structure.

Immediately Crissman, a short distance farther on, opened up. Bullets thudded into the thick planks of the container, burying themselves or splintering the edges. Shawn, realizing his disadvantage, went to all fours and doubled back to where he had been under the stairway. A high mound of trash hindered his view of the alley from there, and still low, he moved past it.

He had not seen where the shots had come from; on the opposite side of the brushy lane along which several small sheds stood, he thought, but he was not sure.

A glass jar somewhere on the crest of the pile, displaced, rolled to the ground and shattered against something solid. Starbuck swore as Cobb Crissman, again aware of his location, drove two quick shots into the mound — both uncomfortably close.

Brushing at the bits of dirt and litter that had showered his face, Starbuck drew back to a place beneath the steps. There was no approach from that angle now; the outlaw had spotted him once again, and would be waiting. But his efforts had not been wasted; the puffs of smoke from Crissman's pistol had betrayed his position.

Cobb was on the opposite side of the alley, and behind one of the sheds — a point that enabled him to keep the area back of the hotel under constant observation. Shawn studied the situation thoughtfully. It might be possible to cross over and work his way up to the outlaw from the other side of the alley. The problem lay in getting there, as he would be forced to expose himself in order to reach the opposite side.

It had to be done; and the means for accomplishing it came to him in that next moment.

Going again to all fours, he returned to the pile of trash. Picking up an empty whiskey bottle, he threw it over the mound. It struck the hard-packed soil in the lane, rolled noisily.

Immediately Crissman fired a shot in the direction of the noise, once more sending up a small geyser of litter. Shawn triggered two quick bullets at the shed in reply, and snatching up another empty bottle from the heap, hurried back to the steps.

Hesitating briefly until he was set, he tossed the glass container over the pile of debris, aiming at the spot where its predecessor had fallen. The clatter drew instant fire from Crissman, and as it sounded, Starbuck rose, raced across the alley to its far side.

The outlaw, intent on the pile of trash and apparently under the impression that he had his adversary pinned down, had not noticed the move. Again reloading, Starbuck circled the first of the sheds, began to make his way along the outer edges of the small weather-worn structures and clumps of rabbitbush and sage. After a few steps he halted, deadened the clink of his spurs with bits of twigs wedged alongside the rowels, and then continued.

The shed behind which the outlaw had stationed himself was just ahead. Shawn paused once more, brushed at the sweat on his face. He knew what lay before him in the next moments — what must be done — and he had no liking for it. But it was not something a man could turn his back on and walk away.

He took another quiet step, a second, and moved away from the shed to where he would have an unobstructed view. The outlaw, attention still on the mound of trash and the area near it, was turned from him.

"Crissman, give it up," Starbuck said softly.

The outlaw whirled. His eyes were wide with surprise, and his leathered features were cut by harsh lines.

"The hell!" he snarled, and brought up his gun.

Starbuck fired once. The outlaw rocked back against the shed from the impact of the heavy bullet coming from such close range. His head sagged forward as he fought to hold the weapon in his stiffening fingers level. And then abruptly he toppled sideways.

21

Starbuck did not move for a long minute, simply stood, eyes on the dead outlaw, pistol still in his hand while smoke trickled from its muzzle. And then a splatter of gunshots in the street snapped him back to the moment.

Pivoting on a heel, he started down the alley at a trot, replacing the spent cartridge in his weapon as he ran. Reaching the rear of the hotel, he hurried along its side wall to the porch, halted, threw his attention into the dusty roadway between the rows of buildings.

Aaron Frisk lay where he had fallen. A short distance from him, Denver Jessel was sprawled face-down in the driving sunlight. Farther over, a second outlaw, Gabe Mather, was slumped against the end post of the hitch rack fronting Purdy's Bakery. He could see a group of men on down the street collected at the side of Jorgenson's. There appeared to be a discussion of some sort underway, and stepping out from the corner of the Yucca Flat, he headed for them.

"Shawn!"

Heather's muffled voice coming from the upper floor of the hotel brought him to a stop. He turned to her. She was at the window where

160

he had seen her earlier, but now alone. He could see the relief in her expression when she saw that he was unharmed. Raising a hand, he waved his reassurance.

The girl struggled briefly with the window, succeeded in raising it a few inches. Bending down, she called, "Is it all over?"

He shook his head. "Not sure. Best you stay inside."

She nodded, straightened up, and he moved on, staying close to the storefronts as he strode along the sidewalk, not inclined to expose himself any more than was necessary. Insofar as he knew, only three of the outlaws were dead, which left a like number unaccounted for; they could be hiding somewhere along the way.

He was aware of persons inside the stores by which he passed, and several times he heard words spoken to him, but coming from behind glass, they were inaudible. He was being blamed by some for the shootout, he suspected, and praised by others for what he had done — but it all amounted to the same. The unfortunate part of it was that it could have been avoided if one man had not lost his head.

Sargent saw him as he angled across the street toward the men. The stable owner's head came up suddenly, and he said something to the others — Jorgenson, Robinette, Pete Barkley, and a couple Shawn did not know. All hurried forward to meet him, Sargent with a tight smile on his lips.

161

"Sure glad to see you!" he said. "We was about to start looking — thinking maybe you'd stopped a bullet when you didn't come back out of the hotel."

"Went after Crissman."

"Seen that. Did you —"

"He's dead in the alley. What about the rest of the bunch?"

"Holed up in my place," Barkley answered in a strained voice, pointing at the general store. "They got my wife! God only knows what —"

"Ain't likely to hurt her, Pete," Robinette said. "Too busy getting set for us."

Such was likely true if the outlaws intended to use the woman as a hostage, Starbuck thought.

"You heard anything from them yet?" he asked.

"Nothing — not a sound," Barkley replied helplessly.

"And you're sure they're all in there?" Shawn continued, studying the building.

It was a low-roofed, sprawling affair with a wide porch across its front, a wagon yard on its north side, and Jorgenson's Feed Store, separated from it by a passageway, to the south. Behind it, not visible from where they were standing, would be an alley and open ground much the same as was the area at the rear of the hotel.

"Seen them all duck in through the door," Norm Robinette answered. "That smart-alec Baker — the one that shot down Frisk — and them two others, Kenshaw and Roanoke. With you getting Crissman and them two dead back there in the street, that takes care of all of them."

"Where's Doc?" Starbuck asked, suddenly aware that one member of his original party was missing. "Hope he didn't run into —"

"He's fine," Sargent said. "Inside his office patching up Charley White. Got hisself nicked coming out of the Border Queen to see what was going on. Ryder wasn't so lucky."

"Dead?"

"Nope, shot up pretty bad, though. Doc ain't sure he'll make it."

"Anybody else?"

"Not that we know of. Folks've been staying under cover ever since things started popping."

"Teague was wounded in the arm," Starbuck said. "Don't know how it happened. Stray bullet, I expect. . . . Be a good idea if we could get word to him and everybody else to keep inside until we finish this thing up."

"When's that?" Barkley demanded worriedly. "When're we going to do something? Can't just stand here talking. We got to get in there, help my wife. . . ."

"We're aiming to, Pete," Jorgenson said. "First need to figure out a way. Don't want to get your missus hurt."

Starbuck nodded his agreement to the feed-store man's words. They had been fortunate so far. None of the men who had backed him from the start had been hurt, and only one of the townspeople was dead — two, if Mason Ryder, the proprietor of the saloon, failed to recover. Now, every care must be taken to see that Pete Barkley's wife went unharmed.

"There only two ways into your place?" he asked, turning to the merchant.

"That's all — front and back doors, unless you count the windows."

"Was talking about rushing them when we seen you coming," Sargent said. "Half of us taking the front, rest the back. Only thing, we're scared we'll get Pete's missus hurt."

"Be too risky for her, all right," Starbuck said, looking off down the street. The smoke had drifted away and the dust settled, and it lay silent and empty except for the dead men waiting in the bright sunlight.

"Backed into a corner like Baker and them others are," Jorgenson said, "they're going to be mighty hard to do anything with."

"How about the roof?" Shawn asked. "There a trapdoor that a man could use to get into the place?"

Barkley frowned, rubbed at his jaw nervously. "Well, yeah, there is. But wouldn't they hear you up there tramping around?"

"Maybe if we start shooting, keep them busy shooting back, they wouldn't notice," Robinette suggested.

"What's wrong with just waiting?" one of the men Starbuck didn't know wondered. "Hell, they got to come out of there sometime."

"Expect that's the answer," Starbuck said. "We wait — see what kind of a deal they want. Right now they're in the driver's seat and can call their shots."

"But my wife — what about her?" Barkley protested in an anguished voice. "Can't just let them —"

"Probably not doing her any harm, but, desperate like they are, if we crowd them, they —"

"You — out there in the street!"

The hail from the store cut into Starbuck's words. He and the men with him quickly turned their attention to Barkley's place.

"We got a woman in here . . ."

"That's the one called Kenshaw," Sargent said.

"She's my wife!" Barkley shouted. "You hurt her, and, by God, I'll —"

"Ease off, mister," Kenshaw broke in. "She ain't going to get hurt none, long as you all do what I tell you."

The storekeeper wheeled to Shawn, his features torn with worry and fear. "What . . . what'll I say?"

"Ask him what they want."

"What do you want us to do?" Barkley called back.

"We're getting out of here — clean out of town. First off, you bring up our horses, tie them to the rack out front. Be a gray and a black and a roan. They're over there at the saloon."

Kenshaw paused. Starbuck said, "We're lis-

165

tening. Go ahead."

"We'll be coming out then — with the woman. She'll be walking in front of me, with my gun pushing in her back. We'll mount up, and I'll be taking her with me on my saddle. You don't try no cute tricks like stopping us, and I'll drop her off at the edge of town. Savvy?"

Starbuck exchanged glances with the men gathered around him. "Don't see that we've got a choice. . . ."

Barkley heaved a heavy sigh. Robinette swore. "Sure don't want to see Pete's missus get hurt, but it's a goddamn shame to let them murderers get away. That Baker ought to hang for cutting down Aaron, way he did."

"The others, too — all of them ought to swing," one of the strangers to Shawn said.

"Maybe we could agree, then have a bunch of us waiting outside town — both ends — and when they've turned Mrs. Barkley loose, open up on them."

"Be afraid to chance it," Starbuck said. "Something could go wrong, tip them off. She'd be the first they'd turn on. Way I figure it, we'd best go along with what they want and hope we'll get a break. That how you all see it?"

Shawn glanced around. The men all nodded. Norm Robinette shrugged. "Like you said, we ain't got much choice."

"Guess we're all agreed, then. We'd better bring up their horses."

Jorgenson said, "I'll go," and turned away.

A thought came to Starbuck. "Get four — the ones they named off, and an extra. If we can get them to put Mrs. Barkley on it, it might help us —"

"What about it?" Kenshaw's voice was loud, impatient.

"We've sent for the horses," Shawn replied. "Be a coupla more minutes."

"Well, get a move on. We ain't waiting all day."

"One thing you'd best get straight," Ross Sargent said. "You hurt that woman, and we'll mount a posse and chase you till doomsday! Want you to remember that!"

"She ain't getting hurt — not as long as you don't try something cute. . . . Where's Cobb? If you've got him locked up somewheres, we want him turned loose, too."

"He's dead," Robinette said. "Along with them other two — Jessel and Mather."

"Cobb's dead?" Kenshaw said with a disbelieving tone. "Who done it?"

"Don't see as it makes any difference now."

"Does to me. I'll be hunting up the jasper that got him, once I'm out of here."

"No need to do any hunting," Starbuck drawled, moving out a step from the other men. "Was me. If you're real anxious to square up for Cobb, as well get at it right now."

"Was you . . . Starbuck?"

"Right. Step out into the street. I'll guarantee these men with me won't cut themselves in. You

167

do the same for Baker and Roanoke — be just the two of us."

The outlaw laughed. "Nope, I ain't about to pull no fool stunt like that — not when I'm holding all the high cards. Be another day."

Jorgenson appeared, moving out from behind the Border Queen and leading four horses. The big man was visible from Barkley's, and Shawn waited for the reaction of Kenshaw when he noted the spare mount.

None came as the feed-store man led the animals up to the hitch rack, wound their reins about the crossbar, and rejoined the others.

"So far so good," Barkley murmured thankfully.

"Now, all of you back off — stand there by the corner of that building, the feed store, so's we can see you good."

Robinette swore angrily. Starbuck shook his head warningly. "Do what he says. Could be we'll get our chance."

The men began to fall back toward Jorgenson's, and Shawn joined them. At once the front door of the general store opened. Mrs. Barkley, a slightly built woman with gray hair, was the first to appear. She nodded to her husband and managed a smile to indicate that she had not been harmed.

Directly behind her, one hand gripping the collar of her dress, the other holding a pistol to her head, was Stinger Kenshaw. Walking at his sides as they crossed the wide porch were the other outlaws — Baker on the left, Job Roanoke to his right.

They came off the landing slowly, taking the steps with care, all watching Starbuck and the men with him closely. Reaching the hitch rack, they halted. Shawn kept his attention on Kenshaw, wondered if he would make use of the extra horse. The outlaw ignored it, and keeping the barrel of his pistol pressed against the woman's head, forced her up and onto the saddle while Baker and Roanoke looked on.

Mrs. Barkley settled, and still not relaxing the weapon in his hand for an instant, Kenshaw thrust a foot into the stirrup and swung up behind her. Glancing then at his two waiting friends, he nodded.

"Climb aboard. . . . Let's get the hell out of here!"

At once Cass Baker and Roanoke stepped to their horses and mounted. All started to wheel away when a sudden commotion alongside the Border Queen brought them about. Alarm rushed through Starbuck. He wheeled. Rufus Teague and a dozen other men, brandishing weapons, totally unaware of the critical situation, were surging into the street.

"Goddamn you — you've double-crossed us!" Stinger Kenshaw yelled.

22

Starbuck's hand was little more than a blur as it came up with the forty-five Colt he carried. He knew without conscious thought that he must shoot fast, else Pete Barkley's wife was a dead woman, and that his aim had to be true or it would be he who was the cause of her death.

The woman screamed as the outlaw jolted from the shock of Shawn's bullet, screamed again as Kenshaw's reflex action triggered the weapon he was clutching. But its muzzle had tipped down, and the leaden slug drove itself harmlessly into the dirt.

The quick hammering of guns was like a drum roll in Starbuck's ears, the men with him opening up on Job Roanoke and Cass Baker. The thunder further increased as the Teague-led party, coming up from the Border Queen at a hard run, began to use their weapons. The air was suddenly filled with drifting smoke and dust, and through it Starbuck saw Kenshaw spilling from the saddle, while Pete Barkley's wife, her mouth blaring in a soundless scream, hair down around her shoulders, was throwing herself from the back of the horse to the ground.

"Martha!" the storekeeper yelled shrilly, and rushed toward her.

In that moment Baker, fighting his frightened horse, twisted half-around, drove a bullet into the man. Pete Barkley threw up his arms, staggered, fell.

On beyond him Roanoke abruptly pitched off his horse, and then Baker, clawing at a shoulder, dropped his weapon and folded over in the saddle. A shout went up from the men with Teague.

"We got 'em . . . we got 'em all!"

Starbuck, grimly silent, with Ross Sargent and Jorgenson at his side, ran to where Barkley lay. The merchant's wife, unhurt from her leap off Kenshaw's mount, was pulling herself upright, features drawn, eyes filled with fear as she stared numbly at her husband.

Reaching Barkley, Shawn knelt beside him, felt for a pulse. There was none. The outlaw's bullet had killed him instantaneously.

"Is . . . is he . . ."

Starbuck glanced up to the woman. He nodded slowly. "I'm sorry."

Mrs. Barkley uttered a high-pitched cry, rushed forward, and dropped to her knees beside her husband. Shawn pulled back, got to his feet.

"I'll go get my old woman," Asa Jorgenson said. "Martha'll need somebody."

Teague and several men were swarming around the fallen outlaws, joyously dragging the bodies of Stinger Kenshaw and Job Roanoke over to the sidewalk, where they were laying them out as if for display. Two others in the

171

party had jerked the wounded Baker upright, handling him with savage brutality.

People were now coming into the street, word having carried quickly to them that it was all over, that the outlaws had been overcome. Glancing over the heads of the nearest, Shawn saw Heather in company with the woman he'd seen in the hotel's window, hurrying toward him.

"String him up now!"

The words cut into Shawn's mind, brought him sharply about. The crowd with Teague had swelled to a score or more, and as he swung to face them, they began to move toward the gallows, carrying Cass Baker with them.

"Wait!" Starbuck yelled.

The crowd, now a mob thirsting for blood, did not hear, but pushed on heedlessly. Shawn glanced hurriedly about. Jorgenson had gone in quest of his wife, that she might give aid and comfort to Martha Barkley. Ross Sargent was kneeling beside the stricken woman in the thickening clouds of dust, endeavoring to console her. Only Norm Robinette was still with him.

"Got to stop this," he said harshly, starting after the mob.

Robinette fell in beside him, and shoulder-to-shoulder they began to break into the steadily growing crowd, forge their way to its center, where the outlaw was being pushed and shoved toward the scaffolding.

"This is a lynching!" Shawn yelled above the

din. "You can't do this!"

"He's got it coming!" a man nearby shouted back. "Shot down Pete Barkley, didn't he? And Aaron Frisk, too!"

"That's right!" another member of the pack added. "Hanging's too good for him! Ought to take a bull whip, cut him to pieces!"

"Drag him!" a different voice suggested. "Scrape all the hide off'n him!"

Using his elbows and the flat of his hands, Shawn fought his way into the circle surrounding Cass Baker. Reaching out, he seized the nearest man by the shoulder, yanked him back.

"You can't do this!"

"The hell we can't!"

"And we're going to!" a heavy-faced redhead added. "Aim to teach these goddamn renegades they can't come into this town and take over, do what they damn please!"

A shoulder drove into Starbuck's ribs, pushing him aside. Men crowded in close, swept Baker beyond his reach. He swore angrily. It was useless to try to stop the mob — he would have to do something else. Glancing back, he located Robinette, still struggling to reach him.

"The gallows!" he shouted. "Only chance we've got!"

Turning away, Shawn began to bull a course through the heaving, swaying pack toward its edge. It took only moments to break clear, and with Robinette beside him, he circled the fringe, gained the steps of the scaffolding, and climbed to the platform.

"Who's got a rope?" someone yelled.

Starbuck drew his pistol, fired a shot into the air. As the confusion below him began to slack off, he triggered his weapon again.

The shifting, struggling mass slowed as it moved up to the framework. Two men pulled free, rushed to mount the stairs. Norm Robinette, his gun out, blocked their way, waved them back. Silence began to settle over the crowd.

"Who're you to say what we can do?" one of the men clutching Cass Baker's arm demanded through the quiet. "We got a right to —"

"You don't have a right to lynch him!" Starbuck shot back. "We go by the law."

"Was you that lynched that other jasper."

"That was a lot different from what you're wanting to do. Forsman had a trial, was sentenced by a judge to hang. He was executed — not lynched."

"All the same thing. This bird here's a murderer, too. We don't have to have no judge tell us to string him up for what he done."

"That's where you're wrong," Starbuck said, raising his voice so that it could be heard above the rumbling of dissatisfaction. "You do have to have a judge. He shot down Pete Barkley in cold blood. I saw him do it. So'd a lot of you, but he still has to be tried and —"

"What's the sense in doing that? Just be going through the motions, and he'll hang anyway."

"It's the law," Starbuck replied, looking out over the crowd. Directly behind the bloodied Baker he saw Rufus Teague. "You know that's the way it has to be, mayor! Get up here with me and make these people see that."

Teague hesitated uncertainly, and then, head down, he moved toward the steps of the gallows.

"You've got to give the law a chance to work," Shawn continued. "This was murder. I don't deny it, but you can't take over and do the job that a judge and jury are intended to do. You do it that way, and there's going to be some innocent men — maybe one of you — lynched one day. Not every murder is as clear-cut as this one. Accidents happen.

"Or there're times when there's no witnesses, and folks will only think — assume — a certain man did the killing. He could be innocent, and if you take the law into your own hands like you're trying to do here, then he'd be the one being murdered. A judge and jury have to hear all the facts and do the deciding whether a man's guilty or not."

"Ain't no doubt about this'n!" a voice shouted from the center of the crowd. "Anyways, country'll be better off with him dead — right along with his partners."

"Not saying you're wrong — only that you've got to first let the law handle it."

Starbuck looked over his shoulder. Rufus Teague, arm bandaged but out of the sling that had been placed about his neck to support it, was beside him. He smiled tightly at the man.

"I've had my say. It's up to you now."

Teague stepped to the front of the gallows platform, looked down upon the now quiet crowd.

"Starbuck's right," he said. "We do this — lynch that man — then we might as well give up trying to build ourselves a decent town."

"That ain't the way you was talking a few minutes ago!" someone challenged.

Teague lowered his glance, nodded. "Lost my head, same as the rest of you, and I'm plenty ashamed — 'specially since it took a stranger to bring me to my senses. But I'm thinking straight now."

"Expect that judge's still over in Casperville," someone volunteered. "Could send for him, hold a trial right away, like that fellow says."

"What we'll do," Teague declared. "Now, couple of you take the prisoner over to the jail and lock him up till I get us a marshal lined up here, then . . ."

Starbuck, moving toward the steps, paused, turned to Teague. "You've got no problem there, mayor. Norm Robinette'll make you a good one."

A puzzled frown pulled at Rufus Teague's features. "Was figuring on you. . . ."

"Me?" Shawn said, surprised.

"Well, yes. Your wife — or I reckon I'd best say your wife-to-be — gave us all to understand you'd like to have the job, along with her taking

176

over the school. Was a committee come to see me, told me that, but if I'm wrong . . ."

"Afraid you are," Starbuck said quietly, and moved on down the stairs.

23

Shawn reached the foot of the steps, halted as Rufus Teague, hurrying across the platform, called out to him. The crowd was still gathered around the scaffolding, and just beyond its fringe he could see Heather standing in a group with several other women.

Three men were hustling Cass Baker off to the jail, and a fourth had sought out Doc Schultz, was conducting him to that office where he could patch up the outlaw's wound and make him fit for trial.

"Can't understand," Teague said. "Was your wife —"

"Not my wife, and I've got no plans to marry," Starbuck said, abruptly impatient. "Mrs. Rustin's a fine woman, and she'll make you a good schoolteacher . . . but we're only friends. Just happened by chance that we were traveling the same direction."

"But she told my wife and the Lucketts . . ." Teague insisted.

"Sorry if the lady gave them the wrong idea. I'm looking for my brother, have been for years, and I won't be settling down until I've found him and straightened out some family business. . . . That's the reason I'm here. Figured this is where he'd be."

"Nobody living here named Starbuck."

"Would've just got here, from Mexico, along with some other folks. I — that is, we, Mrs. Rustin and I — were about a day or so behind them."

"You two are the only travelers that's come into town from down the border way in the last couple of weeks. . . . He must've crossed somewheres else."

"Could've been anywhere," Robinette, now on the lowest step, said.

"He would have been looking for a town. They — there were several people with him — had been held prisoners by the Comancheros, and it's likely some of them got hurt during their escape and needed help."

Robinette nodded thoughtfully. "Well, if they were in this general area, and they didn't cross over and come here, then my guess is they ended up at Perilla — town on west of here in Arizona Territory."

"Was what I'm thinking," Teague said.

"How far west?" Starbuck asked.

"Day's ride, more or less."

Shawn smiled. "Expect I'd best get started, then. Don't want to drop back any farther behind Ben — my brother — than I already am."

Norm Robinette nodded, extended his hand. "Like to shake again and say I'm obliged to you for setting me straight . . . and for recommending me to the mayor for the marshal's job."

"Can figure you've got it," Teague cut in. "I'll swear you in soon's you're ready."

Starbuck glanced up at the older man. "Good choice," he said, and brought his attention back to Norm. "Want to wish you the best of luck."

"Same goes to you," Robinette replied, releasing his grip. "You riding out now?"

"Now," Shawn said, and turning on a heel, moved off through the dispersing crowd to where Heather waited.

He was facing some bad moments with the girl, he knew, and they could be avoided; he had only to ignore her, continue on to Ross Sargent's livery stable, where he'd stalled the sorrel, mount, and ride on. But it was not in him to take the easy way out.

He slowed, came to a stop as she stepped quickly away from the other women, apparently reluctant to have them overhear what would be said, and came forward to meet him. Her features were sober.

"I heard what you told the mayor," she said before he could speak, "I'm sorry, Shawn, I thought we —"

"No need to be," he broke in gently. "If anybody needs to be sorry, I reckon it's me. Want to say now that if I've caused you any shame, I didn't mean to."

"It was my fault. I shouldn't have taken so much for granted. . . . Are you really leaving right away?"

"Soon as I can get my horse. Glad you got

yourself lined up for a job."

"It just happened they were looking for a teacher."

Starbuck reached into a pocket, withdrew two double eagles. His financial condition, thanks to the work he'd found previously in Tombstone, was still good. Palming the coins, he extended his hand and took hers, as if in farewell.

"Want you to take these. You'll need a little cash to get started."

Heather's lips tightened in the way they did when she was displeased. "No, I won't let you —"

"Then we're going to be standing here the rest of the day holding hands," he said, smiling, and then added: "You can figure it for a loan and pay it back the next time I see you."

She gave that a moment's thought. Her eyes softened. "You will be back someday, won't you?"

"Sure," he replied, releasing her. Reaching up, he touched the brim of his hat. "Can't say just when, but we'll meet again. . . . So long."

"Good-bye, Shawn," Heather murmured as he turned away.

Astride the sorrel, an hour later Starbuck was cutting back toward the mountains that lay to the south and west — the Chiricahuas, Ross Sargent had said they were called. Perilla was on the yonder side of them, and while he held no hope of reaching the settlement before dark, he felt a sense of relief in being again on his brother's trail — or at least there was a good possibility that he was.

If Perilla proved to be just another false lead, well, he'd come up empty before many times, and while failure in this particular instance would be hard to take, it would be no novelty. And as in those instances in the past, he'd have no choice but to ride on, resume the search.

Brushing away the sweat on his forehead with the back of a hand, Starbuck narrowed his eyes against the glare and studied the distant blue-gray mountains. He just might make it to Perilla before the day was over, after all.

6/20